THE LIE

"Fastoff cuts with perfend suspense in her latest Ho . . will keep you breathless. .he jaw-dropping end. *The Lie* . . .

Randy Richardson, President Chicago Writers Association

"(*The Lie*) is a must read" book; brilliantly put together displaying details only persons inside law enforcement would know. It is mysterious . . . suspenseful . . . and demonstrates Fastoff's incredible knowledge of the inner workings and jargon used by the FBI and local law enforcement. It keeps you on edge."

Kenneth M. Webb, Jr., President, Fact Finders Group, Inc.

THE PACT

"Once again, JoAnn Fastoff has written a novel that you will find yourself unable to put down in her latest continuation of the Howard Watson Intrigue series."

—Paige Lovitt for *Reader Views*

"Fastoff gives an authentic view of criminal investigation with a touch of believable technology . . . thriller of a story!"

—Detective George Patton (ret.) Chicago Police Dept. & FBI-Chicago Violent Crimes Task Force

"WOW! All I can say is (Fastoff) never lets me down when it comes to action that I can visualize."

—Elliott V. Porter, *Chicago Filmmaker & Actor*

THE GORDIAN KNOT

"A fast-paced and suspenseful novel, enjoyable for diverse readership . . ."

—*Reader Views Shelf*

"I thought I was a seasoned mystery reader. Fastoff has proven me wrong. She put a twist, or was that a turn . . . that delightfully surprised me."

—Sam Rodgers—*Utter Hip Magazine*

Also by JoAnn Fastoff

The Gordian Knot
The Pact
The Lie

THE SMOKE RING

(A Howard Watson Intrigue)

JoAnn Fastoff

authorHOUSE®

AuthorHouse™ LLC
1663 Liberty Drive
Bloomington, IN 47403
www.authorhouse.com
Phone: 1-800-839-8640

Published by AuthorHouse 10/18/2013

ISBN: 978-1-4918-2789-5 (sc)
ISBN: 978-1-4918-2788-8 (e)

Library of Congress Control Number: 2013918601

Any people depicted in stock imagery provided by Thinkstock are models,
and such images are being used for illustrative purposes only.
Certain stock imagery © *Thinkstock.*

This book is printed on acid-free paper.

ACKNOWLEDGMENTS

As always, my writing is dedicated to my offspring Angela and David and my goddaughter Angelita. To my main man Ronny Francis—thanks is truly not enough to repay you for all your effort and all your time. Ronnie Morrison thanks for having my back and dispensing really good "cop" knowledge. Thanks again my "Janet" model, Kim Watts. Thank you Elliott Porter for your terrific insight, advice and knowledge of the film industry! William Dunbar, you always seem to have my back—how is that? Thank you JL Jordan and Adam Jordan Marks, for truly riding with me and holding my hand on this last rollercoaster ride. To the very talented staff at AuthorHouse and especially Julius Artwell; you kept your word again. Armand Scott—thank you for understanding my dream, and making it a reality. To my best friend Dr. Lane Ashmore, you believed in me when I was invisible—I can't say enough . . .

To mom Sarah, *I am the fruit not far from the tree.* NGF—looking down from heaven and smiling? I hope so.

Thank you God for Howard Watson.
JAF

Washington, D.C.

The man knocked on the hotel door again. The body on the floor did not move.

Major General Ronald F. Stacktrain was dead. The blow to his head from hitting the corner of the cocktail table may have assisted in his death.

"Ronny!" he yelled from outside the door. No answer. He knocked on the door again. He yelled again, but still no answer from inside the room. Hotel patrons leaned nervously out their rooms to see who was doing all the yelling. A few called the front desk.

Finally, FBI Special Agent in Charge Howard Watson headed to the hotel's security office to find out why his friend wasn't answering his door.

Two men slipped out of Stacktrain's hotel room once they believed his visitor had departed. They took the stairs to the lobby.

\#

PART ONE

The forecasted beautiful weather in Maryland did not disappoint.

It did however take a backseat to Ronny Stacktrain's funeral. Howard eventually let the tears flow for a dear friend; a dear friend with whom he had played basketball; a dear friend who he watched traverse the Marines from Second Lieutenant to Major General in record time. Ronny was like the younger brother Howard always wanted but God, with his sense of humor, decided he should have sisters instead.

Howard's sons Mark, George and Lawrence were on his right side at the cemetery. His wife Carol was on his left. She placed her hand in his, knowing the touch would keep him from falling apart.

The Watson's had just returned from a two-week vacation in Hawaii when Howard received Ronny's text. Ronny seemed upset. It was as if the information he wanted to share with Howard was too important for an email or a telephone call. He had written, "When you get back in town we have to talk. I'll be at the Capitol Hill Westin, room 810." Now Howard realized why his return texts had gone unanswered.

Howard had rushed to the Westin Hotel after dropping his bags in the hallway at home. He was disappointed in himself for not getting to Ronny's hotel room sooner. He was devastated by Ronny's death. *Why was he in the hotel room? Had someone tried to rob him? Had he known something that led to his death? Why was it so important that he had to see me immediately?* All of these questions were running through his head as he tried to connect the dots. It didn't matter; his friend was not coming back. Howard gave Ronny's casket a military salute before walking to the car. He and his family stopped and hugged Beverly, Ronny's wife, and their two young daughters. Howard promised Beverly and the girls he would find the answers.

Two sets of eyes focused on the funeral procession from inside a black Buick parked a distance from the grave. A flash of sun bounced off the driver's side window and caught Howard's eye. He looked in the direction of the flash. The driver immediately drove the car from the location. *"Paparazzi!"* Still Howard noted the make and color of the car. The Watson family headed home to Virginia. The funeral had erased the two previous weeks of fun.

#

Howard could not answer any of his own questions. *Why Ronny? What happened? Why him?*

According to the D.C. Police report, "(Ronny) was more than likely robbed. Probably a scuffle ensued and he fell and hit his head on the cocktail table on the way to the floor. The thief, or thieves, panicked and ran off. They probably didn't know he died."

Howard could not digest this line of reasoning. No fingerprints, except Ronny's; no money taken, his wallet was still on his body; and no signs of forcible entry. If Ronny was an average American, this scenario might have worked, but Ronny was not average—he was a Major General in the U.S. Marines.

Someone knew who he was. The dresser drawers and bathroom medicine cabinet had been rummaged through. *The thieves must have thought no one was in so Ronny must have surprised them. What were they looking for?* The answers would have to wait until he had a chance to talk to his Chief and ask to sign on to this case.

Across the Potomac, FBI Bureau Section Chief Alberto Marino was discussing Ronald Stacktrain's case with a three star general who wanted the FBI's, *and only the FBI's,* assistance on this matter. Howard was about to get his wish.

#

Ronny Stacktrain had graduated from West Point Academy with a degree in weapons engineering and a minor in French. He became interested in weapons because his father, Marvin, had been one of the few Black weapons experts during the Vietnam War. His dad was Ronny's hero.

Unfortunately, for Marvin, shrapnel claimed the life of his legs while in Vietnam during a tactical weapons training exercise with new recruits. Marvin returned home a hero but paralyzed from the waist down. Ronnie was eight when his father returned home from Vietnam. Although in a wheelchair most of Ronny's life, he never heard his father blame anyone for his injuries nor did he ever miss a beat when talking about the greatness of America. Marvin also never missed a ballgame in which Ronny played, or a track meet in which Ronny ran. He never missed any of Ronny's or his sister's graduations. However, Ronny missed his father's funeral. He and FBI agent Howard Watson were stranded in Siberia on a reconnaissance mission at the time. Ronny recalled how both of them missed funerals of someone dear to them. On that day, he believed he and Howard Watson bonded forever as friends.

#

Ronny became interested in the French language in high school because he overheard a girl with the greatest looking legs he had ever seen telling her locker mate that she was taking French. Ronny would later chase down those legs, date them, and then marry them. It would only take him 10 years to do so.

Despite these inauspicious beginnings, Ronny learned to love the French language. It opened doors to a world he had never known from his modest beginnings as a child from Baltimore. Armed with the French language, Ronny utilized his interpretive skills in various places around the globe: France, Senegal, Ivory Coast, Haiti, Morocco, etc. Whenever she could, his wife Beverly would join him on these adventures. When it came to France, Ronny absolutely loved the wine region, the people and the food, declaring to no one in particular that this was where his pension would be spent.

Wherever he found himself, it was his habit to hang out with the "locals" as much as he could. That way he would always find out what concerned the people on the street. He believed this knowledge would serve him if he decided to later venture into politics. Beverly would always shake her head and say, "Naiveté is a sort of freedom, I guess".

#

Washington, D.C.

The ATF officers were already seated when Howard arrived at Director Alberto Marino's office. Marino wasted no time in introductions. "Special Agents in Charge Richard Cruz and Michael Taylor, I'd like you to meet my Supervising Agent in Charge, Howard Watson". The introductions took only seconds but seemed longer to Howard. He had just put to bed a case that took more than four weeks of his time away from his family. He was suspicious that another major project was about to fall into his lap.

"Agents, what we have here" Marino began, "is the inability of U.S. Governors to make a sound decision regarding cigarette taxes."

Howard looked surprised at his remark. Marino was talking politics. This wasn't his usual style so Howard sensed something was up.

"Agent Cruz" Marino began. "Why don't you tell Agent Watson why you are here?"

Agent Cruz paused for a moment. "Our agency has been tracking tobacco smuggling for the past three years, mainly focusing on three organized gangs in Virginia and North Carolina. Two of the gangs we are certain to shut down within months. This third gang call themselves The Directive, or "The D" for short. We believe this gang is a splinter group broken off from one of the other gangs called The Links. We need to get to the leader. If we can get her . . ."

"It's a woman?" Howard asked in disbelief.

"Yes", Cruz answered. "I know this is hard to swallow, but not only is it a woman, it is a young *Black* woman."

"Smugglers have always been southern white boy organizations" Howard commented. "How did a Black woman slip in?"

Agent Cruz continued. "Agent Watson, we think The D was looking for an "under the radar" type person to work for them. In order to survive, these 21st century tobacco runners had to become equal opportunity employers. The fruit doesn't fall far from the tree. The woman's father and brother have been in and out of California and Arizona prisons more times than we can count for drug manufacturing, delivery, gun running and other associated crimes. Our mark is a little different from the males in her family because as far as we've been able to detect, she does her homework. We're not sure at this time if she's just a front, but we do believe she is smart, *hates us* and doesn't seem too concerned about consequences."

"Wow", Howard exclaimed. "What's her name, and more importantly, why does she hate us?"

"Lorna Hunter" Agent Taylor chimed in, "hails from Los Angeles; here's a picture of her. She hates all law enforcement. Thinks we created her father and brother to do all the negative things they do. I forgot what they call that."

"The Sir Thomas More school of thought," Marino said lazily. "It's written in his book *Utopia*, you know, "first we make thieves, and then we punish them.""

Howard glanced over at Marino with a look that said, "I'm impressed." Marino smiled.

Taylor smiled. "Yeah, that's it. Let me give you some background first. Stop me if you already know this. Tobacco smuggling has been around since Iowa first started taxing tobacco in 1921. The reason other states didn't follow suit immediately was because *even then* it was a contested issue. When you have states like North or South Carolina, which place a measly forty-five cent tax on its cigarettes you're asking for trouble."

"Why?" Howard asked.

"Because Agent Watson, sooner rather than later, the wise guys start coming out of the cracks in the sidewalk bent on making a haul. New York State places a tax on tobacco that is 10 times the amount of the Carolinas tax, which makes theft and smuggling almost a guarantee. Truckers hauling tobacco from Virginia, Kentucky or the Carolinas are 70% certain they will be pulled over by gunpoint or they will run out of gas because someone tapped their gas tanks. They feel they have no recourse but to pretty much let the smugglers take the truck from underneath them. At least they escape with their lives."

Marino spoke. "The thieves then sell all of the cigarettes and tobacco they confiscate to their dealers at a price much higher than the tobacco states, but way lower than New York or Connecticut."

Howard shook his head in disbelief. Cruz added, "A mule probably transports a truckload of 2,000 to 5,000 cartons of cigarettes which can bring in about two million dollars—an unbelievable profit. Then they *easily* sell the stolen cigarettes to the entrepreneurs on the street who sometimes sell one cigarette or "square" at a time. Even these street folks pocket enough for rent and groceries."

Marino spoke again. "Howard, I'd like you and Agent Cruz to work on this case together. I've already contacted Stanton Abrams in Philly to set up his team. Looks like you'll be working with Agents Forrestal and Holloway again. CIA wants to connect with us too as smuggling seems to have cousins in China, Italy and Russia. The teams will meet this Thursday here at headquarters. Make sure everyone is here at 10 am. Get Yamamoto and Waverly off their other cases, ok?"

"Al, that's only three days from now . . . but I'm sure we can work it out."

"Good, we'll see you then."

#

Jimmy Dawson was tired. He had been driving his load south on U.S. Highway 17 for almost 8 hours when he passed the little town of Warrenton, Virginia. That's when he saw the state police lights behind him. "Shit!" was all he could say. *I hope they ain't in a mood for stealing.* He pulled his truck over to the shoulder dialed a number on his cell phone and waited.

Two police officers got out of their patrol car walking on both sides of Jimmy's rig.

"Is this your rig young man?" the officer asked Jimmy. Jimmy noticed the other officer in his side view mirror walking up and down the other side of his semi. "Why yes sir officer, this is my rig."

"Can I see your license son?"

"Can you tell me what I did wrong officer?" Jimmy asked. The cop took a moment before answering. "Why yes I can son, but first I want you to put down that cell phone, step down from your rig and hand me your license and your registration."

Jimmy knew what was coming. "Officer I don't believe I'm going to do that. If you want to write me a ticket for God only knows what, you can do that. But I am not about to step out of my family's bread and butter."

The officer then pulled his gun from its holster and pointed it at Jimmy. The other cop was at the other window, gun also drawn. "Son, either you're gonna step down from your rig or I'm gonna blow out all the tires . . . up to you."

Jimmy stepped down.

One "officer" took Jimmy's cell phone, jumped in his truck and drove away while the other "officer" walked to his police car and drove off in the opposite direction. Jimmy suddenly realized that the police emblem on the car was just a paint job and that his rig and 2,000 cartons of cigarettes had just been stolen.

#

Washington, D.C.

It was Ahmad Waverly's first day back at the Bureau from a two-week vacation in Belize. He glanced at his cell phone and noticed that he had received a text from his Supervisor Tim Yamamoto requesting his presence at a breakfast meeting the next morning at Howard Watson's house. Howard wanted both men to come prepared to discuss cigarette smuggling. Ahmad realized his vacation was over.

Several years prior he had introduced the subject of tobacco trafficking to Tim. It went nowhere *and* he was told to focus his attention on issues like the illicit diamond industry. Ahmad had reluctantly placed tobacco smuggling research on the back burner.

He was elated that the Bureau was finally tackling this ugly subject. He was also curious as to why the *Bureau* was working on a subject near and dear to the heart of the ATF. He figured he would find out soon enough.

After about 15 minutes of "how are you", and "how was vacation" type of conversations, the men tackled the real reason for the meeting. Howard began in between gulps of coffee, "I want you guys to know that Al requested both of you to work with me on this case with ATF and CIA."

"Why?" Tim asked, reaching for a donut. "Because" Howard continued, "we are going to be fighting tobacco . . . specifically cigarette smuggling. And we're talking large scale smuggling Tim, like they did during Prohibition."

Tim and Ahmad glanced at each other longer than they should have which made Howard quickly jump to the point. "I believe my friend Ronny was a casualty of this war. I need you two to help me find out who or what he was battling. In addition, I met with an ATF Supervising Agent yesterday in Al's office who wants us, Virginia FBI and the CIA working as a task force to set up a sting. Also, we will be working with Janet and Gil again from Philadelphia. If you don't think this is enough officers, think again. Maryland State Police has jumped on board. Tim you remember Jim Stanley?" Tim smiled and nodded.

"I already met the ATF guys but you'll meet them on Thursday at a morning meeting in Al's office. I prepared a packet for both of you and assembled from as much research as I could find on tobacco smuggling. Go through it and we'll be up to par with ATF and CIA."

"Tim, if I recall, you did some extensive research a couple of years ago on this very subject. You have anything that you can give me and Ahmad to study?"

"Actually Howard, it was Ahmad's research and it was very thorough. Ahmad was right on target with his prediction that tobacco smuggling would get bigger and costlier if we didn't take notice." Tim glanced over at Ahmad who held in his smile.

"I'll give you what I've got Howard," Ahmad stated. "Although I haven't updated the research in over a year I don't believe it has changed that much." Howard and Tim nodded their heads in agreement.

"Ok guys, I'd like for us to meet back here tomorrow evening to go over what we've got. As Al would say, I don't want ATF and CIA knowing more than we do."

#

"Let me talk to him first so that I know where his head is at," Alberto Marino was saying to the voice on the phone. "No I don't know *for sure* if Stacktrain told him what he was working on. I've given him a couple of weeks to bounce back from his death so I'm sure he'll be upfront with me about anything suspicious that the Major was dealing with. Yeah, I'll talk with you tomorrow General." Marino hung up the phone and stared out his window. There was a knock at the door. Howard opened it slightly and Marino could see his reflection in the glass. "Come in Howard" he said without turning around.

"I know how close you and Major Stacktrain were so I'm just gonna come out and ask."

Howard was somewhat surprised by Al's peculiar tone.

"Did Stacktrain tell you anything about what he was working on before his death?"

"Yes Al, about six or seven months ago. He said he had information on a splinter group working out of Maryland that had ties to a couple of organized tobacco rings in Virginia and North Carolina. He said he would tell me more when he got more information."

"What kind of information?"

"We didn't get that far. All I know is that the group is out of Maryland. Why all the questions Al? What's up?"

"I don't exactly know, but a Three-Star General came to visit and Stacktrain was the subject of the visit."

"What kind of questions did he ask?"

"The usual when someone, *specifically military*, dies suspiciously. You know the questions: what was Stacktrain working on that got him killed; why was he in that hotel; why did he text you before his death? You know questions like that."

If Marino was looking for a rise out of Howard when he mentioned knowing about Ronny's texts, he didn't get it. Instead, he realized Howard was looking for the same answers.

#

PART TWO

"Agents, I am here to talk to you about tobacco smuggling in the US."

Thus began Marino's monologue.

"It has gotten out of hand. To make matters worse China, Russia and Italy now see profitability in this industry. If you hijack a 52-foot truck carrying 5,000 cartons of cigarettes, the hijacker could make millions selling it on the street."

All eyes were glued on Marino.

"The problem is not only that the inventory is being stolen and sold later on the black market. The problem is that the tobacco companies turn a blind eye to the smugglers. In some cases, the tobacco companies have even assisted these smugglers with looting."

Marino glanced over at Richard Cruz, who immediately picked up the baton.

"Me and my partner, Agent Taylor, have been on the case of tobacco and cigarette smuggling for about three years. Unfortunately, we haven't made a dent in their operation. For those of you who aren't familiar with it, this is how it works: the cigarette companies buy the tobacco from the tobacco farmers in order to manufacture the cigarettes. Afterwards the cigarette manufacturer insures the inventory on its way to the wholesale distributor. At this point there is no excise tax stamp on the product. To avoid paying any taxes smugglers divert the cigarettes while in transit."

A hand went up. "How do these entities make their money?"

"Tobacco manufacturers and wholesalers gain from smuggling in several ways: they make their profit when the product is first sold, and subsequently supplies of cheap cigarettes are created (which lowers average prices, boosting demand). Bootleggers or small tobacco rings like The Directive steal small quantities in low tax states and sale in high tax states. Usually the person getting soaked is the independent trucker who is hauling the inventory to a distribution center. So the shipper, in this case the tobacco company, has already been paid and couldn't care less about the theft. Plus they get the insurance money. We call this collusion."

"You may or may not remember several years ago a couple of the big named tobacco giants were finally hauled into court and slapped with some serious fines. Of course serious to us is not necessarily serious to them. Do not misunderstand; we do not believe these companies feel any remorse. In fact, we believe they've learned from any mistakes they made so they don't get caught again. The tobacco smuggling network is organized, but holes do exist. I think with the kind of brain power in this room we can plug up a couple of them."

When the meeting adjourned, Marino asked Howard, Tim and Ahmad to stay.

"Men", Marino began, "this is a big case. We need to find that Hunter woman. We need to know where she goes, where and if she works, what her hobbies are, when she sleeps, who she's dating, and who does she report to? We need this information—not from the CIA, not from the ATF, not even from Philly FBI! Anyone in this room not understanding me?"

No one answered.

"Ok, good. Let's meet later today, say 2 pm. That is all."

#

The driver of Jimmy Dawson's stolen truck pulled off the road near Warrenton, Virginia, into an empty, seemingly abandoned barn. Multiple people seemed to be talking at the same time. The driver of the truck felt the meeting sounded as if it was taking a nasty turn. The young Black woman was telling the five white men that she was in charge and "if you don't think you can deal with this, then get to steppin!" The gathered stopped talking altogether when the driver stepped out of the truck.

The men immediately started unloading the 2,000 cartons of cigarettes. Lorna Hunter made sure of the count before signing the receipt of said delivery. Twenty minutes later the count was complete and correct. The driver after being paid, in cash, hauled ass out of the barn. He dumped the truck some 30 miles away and waited for his partner to pick him up at the location previously agreed upon.

Lorna Hunter made a call on her cell phone. "Yeah, it's me, "she said. "Yeah, everything's here. We need to talk. The voice on the other end wanted to know why. "Because" she said, "you keep sending me idiots who can barely read or write. I need somebody who can actually take directions. Thank you!" She hung up.

Two ATF Agents were one mile away watching through binoculars and listening on audio to the conversations taking place in the barn. One of the agents immediately called Richard Cruz who called Alberto Marino.

#

Lorna Hunter was brought up in Los Angeles. During her first year at UCLA, she lived through the Rodney King "can't we all just get along" joke of a trial. She later suffered through the controversial trial of O. J. Simpson. She was hardened by the thought that "you just can't trust the police."

After graduation from UCLA and armed with a degree in economics, Hunter accepted a job at Howard University in Washington, D.C. because "it was far enough away from Los Angeles but still in the U.S." She moved from the projects and her drug dealing father and brother as quickly as she could. She believed that if her mother were still alive, the life her family was living would surely kill her . . . instead of the cancer that took her young life.

#

Washington, D.C.

Philadelphia FBI Agents Janet Forrestal and Gil Holloway were pleased to be working in D.C. with Howard and his crew again. Howard was equally pleased, however he was still aware of the little matter between Janet and Tim. He was happy with the thought that Tim and his wife Kelly were working out their problems. As a matter of fact, Kelly was pregnant, *finally,* and Tim seemed rather ecstatic about the idea of becoming a father. Howard was just hoping that Janet's presence on this case wouldn't pose any personal problems to the team. He was more than aware of Janet's dedication to the Agency. As a matter of fact, he was instrumental in Janet receiving an accommodation medal on the last mission for saving the lives of two Agents, including Tim.

Still, he had this nagging thought in the back of his mind . . . .

#

At 2 pm the assemblage had gathered in Chief Marino's office.

"Chief", Ahmad was saying as Howard and Tim entered the meeting, "smuggling is widely misunderstood, mostly because exploitation of tax differentials between states is a relatively small part of the problem. In fact, if all the states had exactly the same price and tax structure, smuggling would still continue, just on a smaller scale."

Tim was beaming.

"Thanks for that information Ahmad", Marino continued, "but according to your research what do you believe is the primary cause of tobacco smuggling?"

"There is no primary cause. Smuggling reduces the overall price of cigarettes, consequently increasing demand. The reality is that price is only one of the many factors influencing smuggling. Raising taxes is not the cure. A major problem is the lack of more secure systems for transporting cigarettes. Many countries, including the U.S., fail to treat tobacco smuggling as a serious crime. This makes tobacco more attractive to smugglers who weigh the huge potential for profit against the small chance of being caught, convicted, jailed and/ or fined. Another problem is the existence of a large volume of duty free tobacco and lack of international cooperation. Lastly, smuggling provides cigarettes at a discount to young people and smokers who might otherwise quit smoking because of the high price."

Howard broke in. "We could follow the product to see where it is being diverted".

"You're right Howard" Marino bellowed. "Ahmad, terrific research . . . which is where we start our conversation. Howard I want you and your people to identify someone on your team who can get into The Directive and flush out Lorna Hunter. If we can get to her, maybe with a little convincing she won't follow her father and brother down the same path to prison. We just need a big name to bring down. Is everyone on the same page?" Everyone nodded in agreement.

"Good. We'll talk tomorrow."

Howard looked around the room. "Tim, Ahmad call Janet and Gil, tell them to meet us in my office."

Once gathered in Howard's office the level of excitement became overwhelming. "First", Howard began, "I want all of you to know that Ahmad has produced some excellent research. Unfortunately we have a lot more to do."

Ahmad jumped in, looking at Tim but talking to Howard.

"Howard, with Tim's approval of course, I'd like a chance to get into that cell. I've studied the tracking methods of several smuggling groups, including The Directive, and I believe with some assistance from the ATF I can get into their inner core."

"No way Ahmad" Tim said quickly. "Let's leave breaking into this group's inner circle for the ATF, or even the DEA. I'm not about to let you flap in the wind."

"Tim, I know I can do this. All I . . ."

"Howard, I know it's up to you" Tim grumbled, "but note my objection. We almost lost our lives on our last case and I am not about to even think about Ahmad out there alone. No way, not today."

Howard heaved a sigh. "Tim, think about it. Hunter is looking for someone smart, who can take directions, who is young and who can handle logistics. That someone is Ahmad."

Gil Holloway jumped into the conversation. "Tim, he wouldn't have to be alone. Howard, I'd like to be part of this detail. Forrestal and I worked with the ATF a couple of years ago on a small case involving tobacco trafficking. Although we didn't do any real physical work on the case, we did learn a lot from the ATF research so we know what the environment is like out there."

Howard had to think for a minute. "Gil I'll have to get approval from Abrams for you to join this part of the maneuver. As for you Ahmad, you and Tim have to work this out. I'll agree to whatever decision is made."

"I kind of remember a mail fraud perp a couple of years ago" Janet added, "who said he was with The Directive. Gil and I were supposed to book him but Philly P.D. ended up booking him on something unrelated. For the life of me I can't remember his name. Anyway, the only reason I'm mentioning it is because the guy went to prison but worked with the DA's office to get his sentence reduced. I'm almost certain the name he mentioned was Lorna Hunter. If we can get to this guy maybe he'll play ball with us for info on Hunter."

"Gil" Howard asked, "Do you recall the case?"

"Yeah, I think I do. His name was uh . . . uh . . . Kilpatrick Burns."

"Yes, that's his name" Janet said almost smiling. "If we can find *him* maybe we can learn a little more about Hunter and her crew. The only problem with Burns is that you can't trust him. The story on him is that he will turn in his own mother if it would save his neck."

"We still need him Janet" was all Howard could say.

#

Baltimore, Maryland

Kilpatrick Burns, or Burns to his friends, was born on the wrong side of the tracks. When he made enough money to move to the other side, he maintained the wrong side of the tracks mentality. More money just made more of who he really was . . . in his case, a thug.

Burns could not remember when he wasn't a thief or a liar. His good looks garnered him open invitations to all the parties in high school. Although very smart, he used his intelligence to manipulate people—specifically his teachers and girls. He was once invited to a party in high school where the girl giving the party was, in Burns' words, *"cute, but ultra naïve"*. The party was given in the winter and Burns had heard that the girl's father "had a little bit of money" so he made the girl's family believe that someone had stolen his leather coat at the party.

The girl's parents were beside themselves. The father actually loaned Burns one of his own jackets and drove him home. Unfortunately, for Burns, he never got paid, *and* the coat was never replaced because friends had notified the girl that Burns never wore a coat to the party. When confronted, all Burns could say was *Damn!* This scenario set the stage for the rest of his "lying life".

#

Alberto Marino picked up his ringing phone. "Marino".

The caller at the other end of the line was succinct. "I have information for you on ITC Tobacco."

"What kind of information?" Marino asked.

"The kind you're looking for to put away the bastards killing people with black market money."

"How do I get it and who are you?" Marino asked again.

"Never mind who I am, just meet me at The Twist on Commonwealth Street NW at 9pm. I think what I have for you will get you a promotion Chief. Oh, and another thing, come alone."

Marino stared at the phone for a few seconds after the caller hung up. He immediately had the call traced . . . to a phone booth on Commonwealth Street near The Twist. After weighing his options he called his superior, John Fleischman.

#

John Fleischman was the head of the Violent Crimes Section of the FBI office in Washington, D.C. He absolutely loved his position. He also loved taking credit on a case when sometimes he was nowhere near it. Marino's conversation with "God's Assistant" was going nowhere fast.

"John, the caller knows the case we're working on. I'm just trying to figure out how the information leaked so quickly if it isn't an agent?"

"Al don't leap to any conclusions."

"John, no one on my team leaked this. We've got to move on this. I have to meet this guy and hear what he has to say."

"Al, you aren't going by yourself. You're not a kid anymore; I'm sending someone to watch over you. Or, I'll send someone in your place . . . your choice."

"The person asked for me John; I've got to go. Please don't screw this up."

"Hey, I'm trying to make sure you stick around to use your pension Al. Give me the details."

#

In an abandoned warehouse in the Maryland countryside, Lorna Hunter had called a meeting to talk about a new heist.

"Ok", she began, "this is what is happening right now. The ATF and FBI are on to us. We need some new ideas. All of you are being watched so you've got to check your back. Don't answer questions from someone you don't know. Don't get caught up in someone's politics if you don't know him. If your gut tells you to back up off information—do it. We're being looked at . . . trust me. I need some new blood. I need someone none of you know. I'm working on it."

A hand went up from one of the men.

"Excuse me sir, but what is it that we ain't doin that you need some new blood? Just askin."

She ignored his sarcasm. "I need new blood, Darryl, because you people seem to know little about *know how*. You know, like knowing how to shut your mouth and just listen. City people know how to do that fairly well."

The men looked at each other and grumbled but said nothing out loud. One man leaned into another and whispered "I'd like to stick my *know how* up her arrogant city ass." The other man chuckled.

"Tyson, is there something funny that you would like to share with the rest of us?"

"No sir, I do not wish to share as you might not find it funny."

"Then can we get back to business?"

"Yes sir, we can."

Lorna continued to strategize on the next heist.

#

Arlington, Virginia

Ahmad Waverly was excited about the new case. Tim had not only agreed to allow him to work on the new tobacco smuggling case, but to go undercover to infiltrate Lorna Hunter's gang in Maryland. He was jazzed about the prospect as he made his way to Howard's house to go over major details with him and Gil Holloway. He rang the doorbell and one of Howard's twins answered the door.

"Hello Mr. Waverly" George blurted as if he was in a hurry to be elsewhere. "My dad will be home soon. He asked that you have a seat until he arrives. Mr. Holloway is in the den. My mom will be down in a minute. She wants to know if you want some iced tea or lemonade."

Ahmad could only smile and shake his head no. At that moment Lawrence the other twin, came into the room to ask his brother if he was still going to play the game they were playing before Ahmad interrupted them.

"What are you boys playing?"

"We're playing "Detective Relentless" Lawrence announced. "It's where you have to figure out where the bad guy is hiding after he escapes from jail."

"Wow" Ahmad exclaimed, "Difficult to play?"

"Nah" George answered. "It's a bunch of symbols and numbers your detective has to figure out with clues he gets from his partner. Oh yeah, you only have two minutes to figure it out before the bad guy does a DB Cooper on you. You and Mr. Holloway wanna play a game before Dad gets here?"

"Sure, why not" Ahmad said casually. He looked over at Holloway who shook his head no. Ahmad proceeded to play. For the next 20 minutes, as Holloway watched, Ahmad and the twins were immersed in Detective Relentless.

"I hope I'm not interrupting what looks like torture to you guys" Carol said smiling, "but Howard will be much later than he thought and said for both of you to go home and to meet up with him in the morning."

"Not a problem Carol" Ahmad said. The twins were kicking my *you know what* anyway."

"That's why I didn't play" Holloway said. "I didn't want to be embarrassed by fifth graders."

"Mr. Waverly is almost as good as you, mom" George gushed. "He was just about to catch the bad guy. Maybe next time Mr. Waverly!"

Ahmad smiled and he and Holloway gave both boys the high five before leaving.

#

Baltimore, Maryland

Howard was searching through papers in Ronny Stacktrain's home office. Ronny's wife Beverly was grateful to Howard for going into Ronny's office, since she couldn't bear to enter the room by herself since his death. Howard had no idea what he was looking for, only that he was looking for something—something that might tell him what Ronny knew that got him killed.

Under different circumstances Howard might have believed that Ronny was the victim of a robbery gone wrong, but Howard had been in the business too long to believe in the easy way out. He continued searching through the stacks of folders in Ronny's file cabinet until one file caught his attention. It was filled with unopened letters. The return address on all of the envelopes was from the same place—a post office box located in Silver Spring, Maryland. Also in the file was a writing pad with scribbling. Although he couldn't decipher the notes, a name was understandable— Greg DeWitt.

As he lifted the file out of the cabinet a key fell, clanging when it landed on the hardwood floor. He picked it up, examined it and then called Beverly.

"No Howard" she said as she examined the key. "I've never seen this key before. But then again Ronny always worked in his office with the door closed so he had a lot of secrets. I'm sorry I can't help you with this one."

"Bev, do you mind if I take this key and these letters to headquarters? I might have something . . . maybe."

"Not at all Howard. As a matter of fact, if there is anything else you need in this room—it's yours."

Howard smiled, hugged her and left. He called Marino on his cell phone as soon as he reached his car but got his voicemail instead. *I'll try again in five minutes.*

Five minutes later he tried again. And again. And again. He then called ATF Agent Richard Cruz.

"Any chance you and agent Taylor can meet me at my office in the morning?" I have some notes I pulled from Ronny Stacktrain's files that could be of some value to us . . . or not"

"Sure, but I'll have to see you alone. My partner has an abscessed tooth but was able to get a dental appointment in the morning. Would 10 am be ok?"

"Yeah, that'll work. See you then Agent Cruz."

"Alright but I've got a favor to ask".

"Yeah?"

"Since we're on the same side, call me Rick, ok?"

"Sure Rick, and that's Howard to you."

\#

Marino ditched his security detail by turning at the last minute the wrong way down a one way alley. *The caller said for me to come alone and that's what I am going to do.*

He did, however, have to tell Fleischman where he was headed so he knew someone in the detail would not be far away. Marino recalled "The Twist" as a combination restaurant and bar that lost its appeal some 20 years before, but as he approached the dive he noticed there were at least 10-15 people still eating. He was thinking that they must have felt some loyalty to the place because in his wildest dreams he couldn't imagine the artery-clogging food to be tasteful. He went in, sat at the bar and ordered a Coke. A few minutes later a man sat next to him and suggested they sit in a booth. Marino picked up his glass and headed to an open booth. The stranger sat across from him.

"Chief" he began. "The reason I called you is because I want you to round up two scum lawyers and two judges that are being paid by ITC Tobacco to deport workers who tell authorities about the working abuses at ITC."

"First of all" Marino said, "Where do you get off calling me Chief? Do I know you?"

The man grinned a sinister smile. "No you don't know me now, but you will know of me soon enough. I have the names right here." The man began taking a piece of paper out of his shirt pocket.

"Are you kidding?" Marino asked as he started to rise.

"No Chief, I am not kidding. Please sit down, as you can see I now have a gun pointed at your kneecaps. Please sit down. Don't try calling for help because even if you get it you will still lose your kneecaps".

Marino took a seat. He decided to listen.

#

"It's not like Al not to return a call" Howard was thinking. *It's too late to call him tonight. Maybe he and Ellie went out and he forgot his phone. No way. Al sleeps with that phone.*

"No Howard, you didn't wake me" Ellie answered. "No, Alberto isn't home yet. Do you want me to have him call you when he gets in?'

"No Ellie, I'm sorry to have wakened you. I'll speak to him in the morning. Go back to sleep." With that, both parties ended the call. Howard tried Marino once more. *Voicemail. Something's wrong.* He woke up Tim.

"Something's up with Al. I tried his phone over six times and it goes to voicemail. Ellie says he isn't in yet."

"If it was someone other than Chief, I would say no sweat, but I'm with you Howard, Chief is way too obsessive about his phone. Even when he lost it that one time he called his assistant who called us to tell us he lost it. You say Ellie hasn't heard from him either?"

"She said he called her around 8pm and told her he had to make a run and that he would be home by ten. It's almost eleven—where is he?"

#

Well since you've gotten me here", Marino said gesturing with his glass, "you might as well buy me another Coke." The man smiled and motioned to the waiter. "Good that you see it my way Chief" he said softly.

"What is it that you want Mister . . . ?"

"DeWitt. Gregory DeWitt. I am what people today call a whistleblower. I am . . . was employed for over 10 years with Independent Tobacco Company as a Vice President in HR. We . . . I oversaw what we might call cost effectiveness. I can no longer provide a justification for working for ITC since I have found that most of our farm workers have been afraid to call authorities about the despicable conditions they work under. Some of them have died from heat stroke, pesticide poisoning and other abominations. I believe I have betrayed my moral integrity by ignoring this."

"I don't understand what you want with me?" Marino replied.

"I want you to help me bring this to light."

"Why don't you contact a reputable reporter from the Post or . . . where are you from?"

"Virginia."

"Virginia then."

"I can't Chief Marino. You see I sto . . . took some documents that show ITC has historically hired undocumented labor to keep costs down. It has worked well for them because they can pay them whatever they want to and threaten or punish those who tell anyone with any authority."

Marino took his time. "I still don't know what it is that you seem to think I can help you with?"

"I know you're working on tobacco smuggling right now and I know how ITC operates when it comes to cigarette smuggling. I can completely describe the operation, point you in the direction of The Directive if you help me."

"Why and how do you know we are looking for The Directive?" Marino asked.

"Because I know. Since I finally found my conscience again it's killing me. Those two judges were bought by ITC to make sure the complainers were "legally" deported if they spoke out about abuses on the tobacco plantation. Society needs them gone. Will you help?"

"I don't know. This is really a case for the ATF. Why haven't you contacted them?"

"I have."

"Well?"

"I am working with a rogue agent."

"Don't you think you are putting your life on the line?"

"At this point I don't care . . . seriously. Besides, I have a place to hide now so I'm not too worried about my life. I know that you are highly regarded as an agent and would probably help me or point me in the right direction. Tell me you will at least point me to the right person."

Marino again took his time with his answer. "Call me in my office at 9 am tomorrow. Someone will be in touch. Now if you don't mind, I have to get home." Taking a last swig of his pop, Marino got up from his seat and left the diner.

Once Marino reached the safety of his car, he exhaled deeply. He quickly made two calls on his cell phone, the first one to John Fleischman, the second to Howard. They would meet the next morning in Marino's office.

#

Arlington, Virginia

Carol Watson had known Leonard Ichito since he was eight years old. His aunt and uncle lived across the street from her and Leonard would often visit her sons. Six years later she would reluctantly represent him against his parents when they wanted to move back to Japan and Leonard did not. He felt that since he had been born in the U.S. he was entitled to choose where he wanted to live. Using Carol as his mediator *thanks to her son Mark*, Leonard's parents agreed to let him stay with the aunt and uncle and Carol would be appointed his Power of Attorney for finances. Leonard was required to visit on spring break, summer vacations and the second week of Christmas to celebrate Oshogatsu, the arrival of the New Year, with his parents.

But Leonard saddled Carol with a dilemma. He was about to turn 18 and not only did he want to stay in the U.S. but also wanted to accept the full academic scholarship offered him by Stanford University. Carol almost hyperventilated when she first received the news. She quickly realized that she had to explain this scenario to Leonard's parents, still living in Japan. She did not want to do this. These were the same parents who trusted her with their son's life in the U.S. for four years. The same parents who believed her when she said Leonard would move to Japan after high school graduation to be near them.

But now as she thought back, she was as naïve agreeing to this scenario as Leonard had been promising it. She really felt she had no choice in the matter because Leonard's 18th birthday was less than three months away and according to U.S. laws—he would be considered a liberated teen. She knew she had to act.

#

"Who do you suppose is the rogue?" Howard asked Marino while sifting through a box of donuts.

"Don't know Howard" he answered shaking his head. "It seems our Mr. Greg DeWitt knows but says he's going to lay a trap first. I tried talking him out of it. It won't end well. He seemed adamant. Agent Cruz, I promised him someone would get in touch with him this morning. He seems to know everything you want to know about The Directive. He did however add a caveat—we have to help him put away some wayward judges sewn in the pocket of the ITC Tobacco Company. Let us know how we can help."

"My partner and I will get right on it Chief."

Fleischman walked through the door. "I hope I didn't miss too much?"

"No John" Marino smiled through his words. "You're right on time. I was just telling Agents Watson and Cruz about last night's rendezvous with Greg DeWitt. Seems he found his conscience and now it's eating him up. He wants us to sideline two judges . . . hold on, I have their names right here on the piece of paper he gave me last night."

"He actually had them written down?" Fleischman asked.

"Yeah, he actually did. Also, since he had a gun almost taped to my kneecaps I listened."

"If he had a gun on you we can pick him up now!"

"Can't do that as we need him to identify the operation of The D . . . and soon. Also, he didn't come there to hurt me."

"No?" Fleischman asked. "Then what do you suppose he came there to do?"

"John, he came to unload his guilt."

All eyes were on Marino.

"Guilt's a bitch."

Howard took advantage of the awkward silence in the room. "Al, Agent Cruz and I are going to go over some unopened letters I found in Ronny's file cabinet last night"

"Do you suppose DeWitt and Stacktrain were working on tobacco smuggling?" Fleischman asked.

"I don't know John" Howard answered." I'm guessing that maybe Ronny and DeWitt were working on ITC Tobacco worker fallout. I found a bunch of notes and Greg DeWitt's name was clear."

Marino added, "The three-star general who visited me several days ago wanted to know about DeWitt as well. At the time I had never heard of him; strikes me funny that the Marines are interested in this case."

Fleischman volunteered his services. "Howard, I'm going to contact the Attorney General's office and see what the law will allow using the taxpayer's dollars."

#

Baltimore, Maryland

Janet Forrestal was seated in an undercover surveillance car down the street from a brownstone apartment building. She watched through binoculars as a black Buick pulled up in front of the building and two men got out. The men headed into the building after being buzzed in. Janet noticed that the black Buick fit the description of the vehicle Howard mentioned seeing at Major Stacktrain's funeral.

After waiting a few minutes Forrestal strolled up to the building and noted the names on the bells. One name caught her attention. She returned to the car and immediately called Gil Holloway, her partner, on his cell phone. "Gil, this is Janet. I think I found the black Buick Agent Watson said he saw at Major Stacktrain's funeral. Also, one name on the tenant listing reflects a company name rather than an individual. What do you want me to do?"

"Don't do anything. I'm meeting with Watson in less than an hour and he'll advise us on what to do next. Stay cool . . . good work."

Unbeknownst to Janet two other sets of eyes were also watching the brownstone apartment building.

#

As Howard and Agent Cruz were sifting through the envelopes found in Stacktrain's files, Howard's secretary announced Agents Waverly and Holloway.

"Good you're both here" Howard said. "Help us find something similar in these envelopes."

"What are we looking for Howard?" Ahmad asked.

"Don't know Ahmad, but the reason I couldn't meet you last night was because I was going though Major Stacktrain's files at his house and came across this bunch of unopened letters—all from the same post office box in Silver Spring. Something's here, I just know it."

"Howard" Holloway stated, "Forrestal called me about 40 minutes ago and said she found your black Buick. She took down the VIN number and found out it is registered to a corporation in Baltimore called Zephyr, Inc. And get this, that's the same name on the apartment building that Forrestal was investigating. The corporation's physical address belongs to a warehouse in Silver Spring, Maryland."

"That is good news Gil. Ahmad you and Gil head to Silver Spring. Take this key and find this Post Office box.

Report its contents to me immediately before heading back. Also, get a close look at that warehouse."

"You got it" Ahmad remarked. On their way out the door they almost bumped into Tim Yamamoto; the acknowledgements were brief.

Howard explained everything to Tim up to the point of the letters. All three men began opening the envelopes, trying to truly decipher one (or more?) person's handwriting. A little more than 30 minutes later all three men were exhausted. They couldn't seem to find anything similar in the letters because the handwriting looked more like someone's scribbling. *Maybe it was the rant of a madman?*

Howard's questions to himself would go unanswered. *Why all this note taking? For what purpose? Why and who mailed all these letters to Ronny? Why?* Then it struck him. The surprised look on the other agents' faces made him quickly realize he had said it out loud. "These letters are in code."

#

Maryland State Police Headquarters

He picked up his ringing phone. "Stanley". The voice on the other end of the line got to the point. "We need to meet."

"Why?"

"Because I know why your friend died in that hotel room last month."

"Who is this?"

"Never mind who this is; meet me at the Waverly Lounge on Belkin in 20 minutes. I have information you want badly."

"I can't; I'm in a meeting called by the Director."

"Then your last chance will slip away, won't it?'

"Ok, ok, hold on just a minute. Who are you?"

"Twenty minutes Chief Stanley. And come alone . . . I mean it."

Stanley stared at his phone longer than he should have because 20 minutes was now 19 minutes. He had to make a decision quickly. He didn't know why he believed the caller but he was either in . . . or not.

#

Stanley met Ronny Stacktrain when both attended Howard law school. He and Ronny had been the only students who did not pass their criminal justice enforcement test given *in the first week of school* so they migrated toward each other for that initial reason. Both agreed it would never happen again.

Major transitions happened in their second year. Stanley married his undergraduate sweetheart and Ronny married his high school adoration. Stanley did not return in his last year when his wife's pregnancy required one of them to supply an income. He applied to, and was almost instantly hired by the Brunswick, Maryland Police Department, an agency located 40 miles southwest of the nation's capital.

Ronny went on to finish law school. Stanley attended his hooding ceremony, and both vowed they would litigate together some time in the future. Ronny chuckled, knowing Stanley meant every word. After law school, Ronny changed course and joined the Marines becoming a Second Lieutenant. His first assignment was at FBI headquarters in Quantico, Virginia.

In his rookie year as a police officer, Stanley met FBI Agent Howard Watson when they were forever joined together to save the life of a little boy from kidnappers. The boy was Mark Mason Watson. For the next 10 years Stanley would be invited to major events in Mark's life and felt especially honored when invited to Mark's high school and college graduations. Likewise, the Watson family—Mark, his mother Carol and Howard would be invited to Stanley's law school graduation (at age 35) and later to his promotion ceremony to Chief of Detectives with the Maryland State Police. Stanley considered Howard a true friend and had no problem beating him in their bi-weekly pickup basketball games.

#

Howard was concerned. "Jim, what else did he say to give you any indication that he was telling you the truth?"

"I don't know Howard but he knew that Ronny and I were close friends. I have to meet him. Do you have my back?"

"Tell me where to lay low and I'll be there. Twenty minutes is not a long time but I'll be there."

They now had 17 minutes.

In addition to his friendship with Ronny, Howard had a different motive for getting to the bottom of Ronny's case. Earlier in his life he had a *more than special* friend who died on the job. John Mason served with him in combat and in the FBI Academy. He had been an exceptional FBI agent who got caught in the crossfire of rogue FBI officers. He died a hero bringing down crooked U.S. Senators and several CIA operatives. Howard believed John was looking down from Heaven giving him the thumbs up for saving his wife's and son's life. He also believed John would be happier still knowing he later married his wife and adopted his son. Howard would believe this for the rest of his life.

#

Even though he was a bit of a distance from the Waverly Lounge Howard's FBI-issued binoculars were powerful enough to pick out whatever he wanted to focus on . . . even a person's freckles. He should have told Marino where he was going but he knew Al had enough on his plate just trying to find a D.A. to focus on some possibly wayward judges.

Except for Stanley, Howard didn't see anyone go into the Waverly for the next 15 minutes. He guessed that Jim's caller might have already been at the Waverly when he called.

Stanley returned to his car in less than 15 minutes. Howard waited several more minutes to see if whoever Jim was talking to was also leaving the lounge. No such luck.

Finally when a group did emerge they were all women. Several men went in, but surprisingly no one came out.

He returned to his car and noticed Stanley had called him several times. "Did the guy leave with you?" Howard asked driving off.

"No. I think he was there when he called me. We sat in a booth and he had a gun stuck in my side the whole time we sat down. He must have thought I wasn't coming alone."

"Did he give you any information about Ronny's death that we didn't already know?"

"I would say yes simply because he said Ronny was murdered by ATF agents."

"What?" Howard had to pull over for this explanation. "Who is this guy?"

"He said his name was Greg DeWitt."

"Jim, Al met with this same Greg DeWitt a couple of days ago. He wanted him to enlist his effort in gathering up several scum judges deporting undocumented workers who complained about working conditions at ITC Tobacco. In return DeWitt said he would explain a splinter group's mode of operation regarding cigarette smuggling. He said in the process he would implicate ITC Tobacco."

"This is getting pretty weird Howard. How does DeWitt know about Ronny's death unless he and Ronny were working together?"

"I don't know. What did you tell him?"

"I didn't tell him anything. I simply asked him how it was that he chose me to help him instead of the ATF."

"What did he say?"

"He said he didn't trust them. He wanted me to get in touch with *only* the FBI and ferret out an agent to help with this case. I asked him what case? He said *this case*. He said he needed *this case* resolved so he can go down respectfully."

"What does that mean?"

"I have no idea. But right after he said this he gave me the impression that he suddenly recognized someone in the place. As soon as he was done talking he checked out the back door, which is why you didn't get to see him."

"Did you notice anyone or anything out of the ordinary when you walked in?"

"No, not really; just wondering when the guy was going to show up . . . which was almost instantly, like he knew what I looked like."

#

After being buzzed in the two men climbed the stairs of the brownstone to the second floor and Kilpatrick Burns let them in to the apartment.

"Anybody following you?" he asked the men.

"Nobody that we noticed" one of the men blurted. "Why? Was somebody following us?"

Kilpatrick shook his head in disgust and lead the men into the kitchen where others were waiting. "Alright, listen up" he said to the men. "We have a new job on Tuesday, a company called Parchment Delivery, which means we have only four days to get our act together."

"Where's it coming from?" someone asked.

"Vaughn, Virginia. Some place near nowhere, Virginia. The truck will be carrying 5,000 this time."

Two ATF agents seated a block away in an undercover surveillance vehicle were listening to the complete conversation. One immediately called Agent Cruz on his cell phone to report the conversation.

#

After finally figuring out that the letters might be written in code, all three agents resigned themselves to the fact that they could not even begin to tackle such a task. "We'll have to turn to the CIA" Howard said, "and see if their decoder can break the code."

"Howard?" Tim asked, "What about Allen Knox? Remember the operative that worked on the diamond smuggling case with us?"

"Good one Tim! God only knows where he is and what he's working on, but I'll check with Al and see if we can enlist him or his people."

"Who's Allen Knox?" Cruz asked.

Tim smiled. "He's an operative that assumed an alias as a diamond dealer in Miami to work with us on an illegal diamond smuggling case a couple of months ago. If it hadn't been for Janet . . . Agent Forrestal, Knox and I wouldn't have escaped with our lives. Anyway, Knox turned out to be a really cool dude . . . and very smart."

"Now that we know we can't make heads nor tails out of these letters" Howard stated, "I'll have to get with Al and see what he can do."

Cruz answered his cell phone. "That's good news. How long will it take you to get here?" Looking at Howard he said on the phone, "Why don't you meet me at Agent Watson's office in an hour and we can all hear the conversation? Good work, see you then."

"Agent Watson . . ."

"Howard."

"Howard, my men picked up complete audio from the brownstone Agent Forrestal was staking out in Baltimore. They learned about the next heist by The D. They're bringing the recording so we can review it. Maybe we can grab some lunch and meet them back here in an hour?"

"Sounds good. Tim, join us."

#

Ahmad and Holloway found the post office box in Silver Spring, Maryland. Ahmad called Howard as Holloway drove them back to D.C. "Howard, it's a shoebox size container. Do you want me to open it?"

"No Ahmad! Anything ticking or any strange smell emanating from the box? How much does it weigh?"

"No Howard, nothing's ticking. The box is very light, like maybe with papers inside. But we are on our way back."

Howard turned to Tim. "Explain the situation to the bomb squad and then have them go to the storage facility in 40 minutes."

Marino located CIA Operative Allen Knox—in Argentina. He explained the case they were working on (not in great detail) and the letters and the types of codes and symbols on the letters that Howard had found in Ronny Stacktrain's office. Knox agreed to help out but couldn't leave Argentina for at least four days. Could Marino wait? If not, he could give him two operatives' names that could probably decipher, or at the very least take a look at the code and, in fact, make sure it really was a code. Would this work?"

Marino told Knox he would wait for him to return to the States.

Knox had one last question. *Is Agent Forrestal working on this case with D.C.?*

#

Howard and his team, Janet, Gil and ATF Agents Richard Cruz and swollen-jawed Michael Taylor were gathered in Howard's office exchanging ideas on a course of action when Marino walked in.

"I hope I haven't missed anything?"

"No Chief" Howard said as he motioned to him to sit at his desk. "As a matter of fact you're just in time. We're waiting for several of Agent Cruz's men to show up with info on The D's next move."

Just then Howard's secretary announced that the bomb squadron was ready. Marino looked surprised; Howard filled him in.

The facility storage area was located across the Potomac River in a wooded area. The possibly destructive material was evaluated by two personnel who were outfitted in headgear, padded clothing and excessively thick gloves. Ten minutes later one of the men called Howard's cell phone.

"Two DVD's."

Although they were thanked profusely, the personnel were grateful the box did not pose a threat to life or limb. The bomb squad agreed to deliver the box later. Meanwhile, Cruz's ATF officers arrived. Marino suggested the meeting move to Howard's conference room down the hall. Once inside Holloway provided a report on the visit to the warehouse:

"Although completely lacking in equipment, furniture and any other necessities that would suggest a corporate body at work, there were signs of recent activity. Ahmad and I uncovered evidence of someone smoking as we found cigarette butts along with a Styrofoam cup with a trace of rye whiskey. We also looked for tread marks—there were none. We deduced that someone erased them before we got there. We don't know how they knew we were coming. The warehouse is in need of repair as the roof has several large holes in it and none of the doors actually close. I'd say the building is just a front in order to comply with the law."

Marino looked pleased with the report. "Good work Holloway." Holloway smiled. Just then the bomb squadron arrived.

"Agent Watson, we decided to save you some time." Ahmad took the box and thanked the men . . . again. Howard then asked Ahmad to set up the audio cassette machine in order to listen to the conversation the ATF recorded from the brownstone.

Forty minutes later the audio recording finished.

"Okay" Howard began. "We now know that The D is about to confiscate another truck from the ITC plant in Vaughn, Virginia. Looking on this map it looks like it's a little more than 100 miles from Baltimore."

"Those are some hard miles Howard" Marino interjected. "They're over the Shenandoah Valley/Blue Ridge area."

"That's right Chief. So if we can arrange to get our team into a decoy truck at Vaughn, The D should not be too far behind. I realize that it's mountainous terrain but Ahmad and his team can come up with some type of GPS tracking system that would not only make clear the stolen trucks' exact location but would tell us the most efficient way to get to that truck to apprehend the drivers. Ahmad can you do that?"

"Wow Howard, I think you have me mixed up with the Great and Powerful Oz."

#

Lorna Hunter was seated in a booth in a restaurant looking at a breakfast menu when the man sat down across from her.

"We have a problem; don't say anything" he whispered. "A decoy truck is scheduled to leave Vaughn before the real

Parchment truck is due to leave the plant. We're being set up so I say we scrub this job for now."

"I say we still hit the real truck, just later. Also, two men quit on me so I need to hire somebody . . . that is if we want the jobs to run smoother."

"Have them checked out first."

She looked displeased with his statement.

After contemplating her suggestion he said "Ok, let's still do the Parchment job."

"Sounds good to me!"

"By the way", he added, "I think DeWitt is going to roll over on us".

"Why? What gives?"

"He's working as an informant for the FBI and hasn't returned my calls or texts for the past week. One of my plants said he saw him in a club on Belkin the other night talking to Maryland State Police."

"Maybe they're friends."

"I doubt it. My guy said when DeWitt saw him he left the club."

"Did the MSP follow?"

"Not right away. I'll check it out. We don't need anyone sweatin' us. So you're saying that your team is in place for Tuesday at Parchment?"

"Absolutely."

"Okay, we'll talk about the Kilgallen job after this."

The man got up and left the diner. Hunter returned to reading the menu.

#

While Leonard dialed the phone number to his parent's house in Japan, his aunt and uncle *and* Carol sat on the sofa, motionless. He spoke in Japanese to his parents and although Carol did not understand Japanese she knew by the tone of Leonard's voice and the heads bowed on the couch beside her that the conversation had gone downhill. A few minutes later Leonard attempted to hand the phone to his aunt . . . who did not wish to speak.

Carol suddenly felt like a child waiting for her father to get home to hear bad news about her from her mother. She had had enough. Mustering up every ounce of courage she took the phone from Leonard while giving him the *I'll deal with you later* look and spoke to his parents.

Later, when she would repeat this story to her family over dinner, she would say that the Ichito's didn't seem that terribly upset. As a matter of fact they seemed almost eerily okay with Leonard's decision. Maybe, she thought, they had reconciled themselves, perhaps even months ago or longer, that Leonard would want to stay in the United States. Still, "they were not pleased with him" she said, "because he should have done the honorable thing by telling them he had applied to the colleges". On the other hand, she thought, they were quite pleased that Leonard had won a full scholarship to a fine university such as Stanford.

#

It took Howard's team more than a day to hash out the details with ITC Tobacco personnel regarding the sting operation. It was decided that Holloway and Ahmad would rotate behind the wheel of the decoy truck. Cruz and Taylor would be in an unmarked white truck 10 miles east of the plant. Howard, Tim and Janet would be in another unmarked truck 10 miles east of Cruz and Taylor.

All agents were armed. Holloway and Ahmad's weapons were fastened around their ankles. After 60 minutes on the road Ahmad called Tim. "Anything?" he asked.

"No Ahmad . . . nothing yet. Give it 30 more miles. At that time we'll assume our plan has been discovered."

"Okay Tim."

Forty-five minutes later Gil and Ahmad had reached Highway 64, which meant only 40 minutes to Baltimore. It was at that time that they were informed that the real Parchment truck had been hijacked 60 minutes *after* their departure from the plant. But by whom? Someone at ITC? The team returned to D.C. with questions that would go unanswered for at least 12 hours.

#

The next morning everyone was in Marino's office when Fleischman stomped in. "I want answers and I want them today!" He bellowed.

Marino tried to offer a possible explanation but Fleischman was not listening. "I want to meet this guy DeWitt. Al, I also want to meet with you and MSP Stanley from Baltimore before we meet with DeWitt. I want to know what DeWitt knows. And I'll just bet he knew about this fiasco."

Marino could only defer to the demands of his superior.

#

For two days the teams searched for DeWitt, with no luck. Forrestal and Holloway stationed themselves at the two establishments in which DeWitt met Marino and Stanley—still no luck. He was in hiding, but from whom? On the third day DeWitt phoned Marino.

"Looking for me?" he asked slyly.

"Yes" Marino answered calmly. "We'd like to meet with you, wherever you say."

"Are you going to look into the charges we talked about for ITC?"

"Yes."

"Good. I know you're a man of your word so let's get down to business. When do you want to meet and what will we be talking about?"

"What about tomorrow, say 2 pm in my off . . ."

"No. I can't come there. You'll have to meet me in Maryland."

"Okay; where in Maryland?"

"Silver Spring. There's a restaurant there called the Tobacco Leaf. It's a dive but the food is good. Be there at 9 am. Bring Stanley from MSP with you. No one else understand?"

"My superior who might be instrumental with the Attorney General's office wants to be included in this meeting. Can we bring him?"

"What's his name?"

"John Fleischman."

"Never heard of him. Do you trust him?"

"Yes."

"Alright, tomorrow at 9am." He hung up.

Marino had the call traced to a land number. He immediately called the GPS division and had the unit trace the location of the call. He then phoned Stanley and Howard. Afterwards he reluctantly contacted Fleischman. Once he hung up with Fleischman the GPS unit called and told him the cell phone was located at the Michigan Motel in Sandy Spring, Maryland room 321. The motel was just off Highway 108, about 45 minutes north of D.C.

So Marino now knew where Dewitt was laying low.

#

Howard was puzzled by the turn of events. Could someone on the task force have leaked this information? And could the leak be working with ITC Tobacco Company? *A bigger question—who?* He needed to talk to Marino . . . alone. He needed Marino to understand that DeWitt knows who the leak is and if Fleischman doesn't deliver on the promise of a full scale investigation into ITC, his peoples' lives could be in peril. He must make Marino recognize the seriousness of what he feared was John's empty promise.

But first he needed to talk to Tim.

\#

"I don't know Howard" Tim was saying. "What if it's Agent Cruz? He knows everything . . . how smuggling works . . . all the details . . . hell, he came up with some of them!"

"Maybe. I'm wondering if we should rule out Taylor 'cause he hasn't been around that much. It could even be one of Cruz's other guys". "I just don't want it to be Janet or Gil. That would be a hard pill to swallow."

Tim could not be more adamant. "Howard, no way is Janet involved! No way."

Howard took an unyielding stance. "We have to plug up the leak if we're to continue."

"If you don't mind Howard I'd like to ask Ahmad some questions about Holloway without his flag going up. Is that ok with you?"

"Sure, even though we know it isn't Ahmad, I still don't want others in on this setback at this time."

Tim caught up with Ahmad later in the day. "What's your opinion of Holloway," he said offhandedly, "since you worked with him on the diamond smuggling case in Miami, rode with him to Silver Spring and were in on the ITC sting?"

"None really. He always has a bunch of questions but seems onboard—ready for any outcome. Why? What's up?"

"Nothing. I just want to make sure you believe he has your back on this maneuver."

"You're acting like my mother Tim. Stop it."

#

Howard also wanted to know the same answer. "Ahmad, The Great and Powerful Oz, how do we proceed?"

While recognizing the urgency of what was being asked, the only thing Ahmad could say was "I don't know."

#

Silver Spring, Maryland

The drive to the Tobacco Leaf restaurant was at least 20 minutes but the three men being chauffeured in the Lincoln never uttered a word. Marino had been schooled by Howard that there appeared to be a leak so he decided on verbal caution even if it meant silence. He did however have a conversation with Jim Stanley on taking the lead. Stanley seemed okay with the reconfiguration of authority, but felt Fleischman was going to be a problem as he had already decided that DeWitt should be thrown into federal prison. Marino hoped Fleischman had already talked to the Attorney General's office.

The diner was small but clean. DeWitt was already seated at a table so the men grabbed seats and ordered coffee. Only one person seemed to be in a hurry to hear what Greg DeWitt had to say. That one person would be John Fleischman.

#

"We need a tracking system" Howard was saying. "That will allow us to monitor the movement of a certain delivery of cigarettes before the shipment is diverted. This system should be able to trace the product by its marking or some type of code on the packs."

While Ahmad was weighing the complications of such an idea, Tim asked "You mean follow the product like scientists do with animals in the wild?"

"Yes Tim."

"The only problem I see" Tim said shaking his head, "is that ITC might be a partner in their own robbery. How do we go around them?"

Howard admitted there were problems to work out. "But if Dewitt is really going to help us, he should be able to tell us who inside ITC can be trusted to mark or code our product?"

#

"We can't deliver all of those requests" Fleischman was saying to DeWitt. "I just can't guarantee that the judges will go down. I'll say it again, the only promise that I can keep is getting you your meeting with the Attorney General's office."

"I don't know if I trust you Mr . . . ."

"Agent."

"*Agent* Fleischman. Okay, I know what I'll do. I'll send a different page of the operation of The Directive to you daily by email. Page one says a Black woman named Hunter has her troops ready to hit a Warrenton Tobacco truck leaving at 9am from their plant on Friday. You'll get page two tomorrow."

"Why don't you just give us all the information at once, DeWitt? Why these games?" Fleischman asked.

"Because *Agent* Fleischman, until I actually see you keeping your word, I'll keep slipping you the information you need page by page . . . day by day. I'm guessing we will end up at the finish line at the same time. It's up to you how quickly we get there."

Jim Stanley finally spoke. "Mr. DeWitt, how is that you know about Major Stacktrain's death?"

"You mean Ron's murder in the Westin?"

"Yes."

"I was supposed to meet with him and an FBI Agent named Watson the day of his death. Ron said I could trust Watson. I was going to expose ITC Tobacco's working conditions to the press and Ron was going to introduce me to a reporter that would run the story at the Post. Unfortunately, I got to his hotel too late. I figured whoever killed Ron wants me dead too."

Stanley continued. "Why did they go through his personal belongings at the hotel? What were they looking for?"

"They were looking for complaint documents about ITC not knowing that *I had them on me* and was bringing them to the reporter. I know they're looking for me now; that's why I went underground."

"What happened to the reporter? Marino asked.

"I don't know. Actually I don't know if the reporter was legit or part of the setup."

"Did you meet Agent Watson?"

"No, but as I was coming off the elevator I believe it was him banging on Ron's door. Before I was able to speak to him he walked off in the other direction to security, I suppose. I looked him up and found out he works for *you* Chief Marino, which is why I called you."

Marino leaned into Dewitt. "Mr. DeWitt, Agent Fleischman is going to fulfill your request . . . but let me say this; you don't want to go up against me if one of my agents gets hurt. Betrayal after trust is deadly." He then leaned back in his seat.

"Chief Marino, no one knows this better than I do. Look for an email tomorrow."

With that said Marino got up, threw a twenty dollar bill on the table and both parties went their separate ways.

#

Howard was of the belief that someone knew everything he and the team talked about. Someone knew Ronny Stacktrain. Someone believed Ronny had information of importance. Sadly, Ronny knew the someone he let into his hotel room. This same someone knew about the sting operation at ITC Tobacco. *Who is it? Is it Holloway? Cruz? Michael Taylor? Certainly not Fleischman or Marino. Certainly not Jim Stanley.*

He didn't know Gil like he knew Janet but Stanton Abrams knew them both and trusted them both. He trusted Stanton but still, "power tends to corrupt . . ."

Once he had succumbed to the fact that there was a leak, he began scaling back on supplying information to everyone . . . including Gil Holloway and Janet Forrestal. In his heart he didn't want to believe Janet was the leak. But in this business, which included betrayal, he couldn't be sure.

I have to get to the bottom of this. Allen Knox will be of great help.

#

"I was most intrigued by your text Agent Watson. Leak is a strong word. What makes you believe this is going on?" CIA Operative Allen Knox had more than a few questions.

"I believe it Knox because too many undisclosed strategies have been compromised." He then went on to name them.

"Well we can certainly lay a trap for whoever it is but you have to know that it will get ugly trying to rule out the infiltrator. There's an old saying that sprung up during WWII's double-agent days and is still valid today: "A soldier working both sides of the battle cannot be trusted on either side." This person is out for himself or herself, but c'mon Watson, you can't be serious about Agent Forrestal?"

"I've exhausted all my options Knox so I can't leave any stone unturned. By the way, only you, Chief Marino and I will know this plan."

"Ok then, I have an idea."

#

Reston, Virginia

Lorna Hunter was at her bedroom desk fingering a picture of her with her late mother when her apartment doorbell buzzed. She peeked out of the curtain window of her second floor apartment to see two men ringing her bell and looking up toward her window. She ducked back from the window. *They know where I live!* She did not answer the bell. Nor did she answer it on the second and third buzz. The two men then walked down the block looking at parked cars. She was almost overjoyed knowing that her car was in the garage behind her building. Since her name wasn't on the bell she was wondering how her father and brother found her. *They must want or need something. That's the only reason they would be coming around.*

The two men came back to her building, looked around then got into a late model BMW and drove off slowly. She watched as the car traveled down the street and then out of sight. She was thinking that now she has to be really careful or else they'll want a piece of the action and screw it up for everyone! *How did they find me?*

She decided to make a call. "It's me. My father and brother are in town for God only knows what and . . ."

The male voice at the other end cut her off. "Do you need them to leave and go back to California?"

"Yes, but I don't want them hurt, understand?"

"This poses a problem for me."

"I don't care. Tell them they're not welcome and pay them off."

"Okay, whatever you say. What if they don't want the money? What if they actually came to see you?"

"My father doesn't visit. He also never plans anything— things just happen. My brother is my father in a younger body. They need something, like money or a place to hide out . . . or whatever. Just get rid of them."

"Ok." He said.

She ended the call.

I just don't understand how those two can get me so unhinged. She then began pacing across her apartment.

#

Other than Howard and Marino no one else knew Allen Knox was back in the States. Knox had taken a look at the so-called scribbling in the letters that Howard had found in Stacktrain's files. He decided that yes, they were in code but he would have to contact a colleague for assistance in decoding the letters.

The other members on Howard's team were told that Knox was sidelined in Argentina so they would have to find another operative to work on decoding the letters.

Ahmad and his crew moved on to the more exciting work of viewing the DVD's.

#

Knox surprised DeWitt at his Michigan Motel hideout in Sandy Spring, Maryland.

"Who are you?" he demanded while looking in both directions outside his door.

"Let just say" Knox said as he let himself into DeWitt's room, "that unlike Marino and his people I'm not here to dicker with you on page by page issues."

"What is it that you want? Who sent you?"

"Never mind who sent me. Sit down DeWitt, we need to talk. I need to know which tobacco plant will be hit next Friday?"

"I . . . don't know what you mean?"

Just then Knox took a knife from around his ankle and asked DeWitt for the last time "Which tobacco plant will be hit next Friday?"

"I still . . . don't know what you mean?"

Knox then grabbed DeWitt by the throat and held the knife on one of his eyelids. "DeWitt, I can be the last person you will ever see with this eye or you can help me out—up to you. Remember, seemed easy enough for me to find you so I'm wondering how long you think it will take for your real enemies to catch up to you?"

#

Washington, D.C.

The teams were gathered in Howard's conference room. "Okay, we missed an important opportunity with the Parchment hijacking. We were naïve but we won't miss a step with the Warrenton truck scheduled for next Friday."

A hand went up in the room. "Agent Watson, what makes you so sure about Warrenton? I mean, how do we know whoever was on to us won't know this too?"

"We're sure. But glad you asked Agent Taylor. Yamamoto has more concise logistics worked out this time."

Tim took the cue. "We are going to place crews at the two entrances the night before, instead of getting in place the morning of. Ahmad's unit is working on a tracking device which will accelerate the time to find the truck. We'll have two men in place at the Warrenton plant posing as employees so we'll know exactly when those trucks are heading out. No decoy trucks this time, only our surveillance trucks."

Another hand went up. "How will our people know which truck is going to be hijacked?"

"They don't know Gil, because there will be two trucks leaving that morning and we will be following both trucks."

Howard took over. "Okay; we have five days to get this in place correctly. Let's meet here again at 3pm and go over logistics with everyone. Everybody clear?"

All heads were nodding.

"Good, see you then."

Ahmad entered the office as the others were leaving. Once they were all out of earshot he informed Howard and Tim that the DVD's were blank.

#

Kelly Yamamoto was four months pregnant. This time she waited until Tim gave her the "go ahead sign" to tell the families. Today she and her older sister and Carol Watson were shopping for baby stuff. She was so excited she didn't realize that she was almost giddy. Her sister brought it to her attention in a big way. "Stop it!" was all she had to say and Kelly became restrained . . . sort of.

It had been ten years since she and Tim said "I do" and she had wanted babies from the start. Even though Tim did not share in her enthusiasm for children, she thought she could eventually break him down. Unfortunately it did not happen. Ten years later the relationship was crumbling. She was just about to give up on the marriage when Tim called her while on assignment begging her not to leave. She didn't know what the circumstances were which compelled him to call, nor would she ever ask, but suffice it to say whatever it was, he came home a changed man.

#

Allen Knox sent Janet a text. He knew that only Marino and Watson were supposed to know he was in the States. He knew by reaching out to her and blowing his cover that his 15 year career as an operative could go down the drain. He knew there could be consequences in his calling her; he knew there could be complications; he knew all this yet he still wanted to see her.

Four months prior when their combined task force assignment wrapped up in Miami he asked Janet to dinner. The conversation and evening could not have gone better. It's when he asked her out again that she declined. She told him that the timing could not have been worse.

Janet found out that her real father, whom she was told had died in Viet Nam, was actually a former disgraced FBI agent who died while delivering illicit diamonds during a deal gone wrong. Because of this lie, she could not bring herself to speak to her mother or adopted father for weeks. Her Supervising Agent in Charge honored her request for time off, giving her 30 days to get her head straight. She used this time to travel to Morocco and Egypt and reflect on the lie she had been told.

After her month away she decided to trust in God. Shortly after returning to the states she sat down with her mother and father and had a heart to heart talk about moving forward. It was then that she thought about Knox. It was a towering thought. She didn't know what kind of an assignment he was on or where he was in the world or if he was seeing someone or . . . how he still felt about her.

She thought back about his offer for dinner and she felt somewhat relieved that her family drama got in the way. She figured if she was going to be honest with herself she would admit that she really didn't want to strike up a relationship with someone in the field, or someone whom she might not see for stretches of time, or someone who might have secrets, or even someone who might end up dead. She just didn't think it was a positive way to begin a relationship.

But if she were to be completely honest with herself . . .

She texted him back. "Yes I'll meet you. Where and when?"

#

Ahmad was in the lab busy putting the finishing touches on his newest invention. He was humming to a Rolling Stones song playing on the satellite radio and was a little startled when he turned around to see Tim standing there.

"I need to say something."

Ahmad turned off the radio.

"I'm sorry for the incident that occurred the other day. I don't want you to ever think I don't have confidence in your skills as an agent. For a moment I was flushed with the feeling of mortality and that you would be out there alone . . ."

Ahmad cut him off. "Tim, you don't have to apologize. I know the routine and I have gone over it in my head time and time again. Remember when I first met Howard? It was because of the death of John Mason. I saw the look in Howard's eyes when he lost his best friend, his colleague, his buddy. Now he's lost another friend in Ronny. It's a heavy burden on him and I want to help him in every way that I can. I saw that same look in your eyes. We both know what this job asks of us. We both signed on to never jump before we know the depth of what we are jumping over or into. The job comes with highs and lows. As long as you and Howard have my back, I know it's still intact."

Then, with almost childlike glee, Ahmad asked, "Now can I show you what I've got?"

#

"What do you mean they need to see me?" Lorna screamed on the phone. "I have business that requires all of my focus right now and I don't need my father or my brother interfering. How did they find out where I was?"

"Seems one of your defectors shared a jail cell with your father a couple of months ago in an Arizona prison; small world." The voice on the phone continued. "I guess your old man just got out and probably wants to rekindle his relationship with his estranged daughter."

"Why was he in an Arizona prison?" she asked.

"Got caught smuggling coke from Mexico trying to get to L.A. by going through Yuma."

"What?!!"

"According to my source he and his posse thought that if they could go through the mountains they had a chance."

"With the Border Patrol stationed all over the complete state? Stupid. Stupid. Stupid!"

"What do you want me to do? They're not gonna leave quietly."

"I'll take a meeting with them. I have to get rid of them . . . I have to."

"You got it."

#

Ahmad was anxious to show Howard his new pet—a miniscule transparent semiconductor chip which he named SPOT—Satellite Positioning Object Tracker.

"We can place this wafer on and in anything, and it can't be destroyed by water, except salt water, or fire. It can't be frozen or burned or broken or bent. Look I'll show you."

With that he tried to burn the wafer with a cigarette lighter but it didn't melt. He stomped on it with the heel of his boot and the material didn't reveal any damage.

"Not only can we follow whoever or whatever is transporting whoever or whatever, we can also zoom in on the location to within a couple of meters. If Spot was on a person, we would quickly be able to find out the exact address of the location even in a 50 story apartment building with 400 apartments in the building. We would, sorry to say, have a little bit of trouble finding Spot if he was digested.

Even though he won't hurt or do damage to our body, he will dissolve in about 12 hours because of the salt and acids."

"Howard, I'm giving you and Tim this specially designed recorder that will be a sort of leash on Spot. Wherever he roams he won't get far. Unfortunately it is only text so you won't be able to see person, place or thing."

"Sounds terrific Ahmad, but what's the downside?"

"The chip can only last 72 hours."

"What? Three days?"

"Howard" Tim quickly added, "Ahmad and his crew are working feverishly to extend the chip's life but at this time that's all we can get out of it without any device recognizing the chip. This means no scanner of any type, even at the airport, will pick up the chip unless it is 72.1 hours old."

Ahmad added, "Also if Spot is being transported underground like in a subway, underground garage or under the water, it will be difficult to follow until he reemerges above ground. The satellite can only follow it above ground."

"Great work Ahmad, but we now have to plan our detail to the precise minute in order to make sure you and Gil place the chip . . ."

"Spot" Ahmad said correcting him.

. . . "Make sure you and Gil place Spot in the cigarette cartons going into the correct truck that will hopefully be picked up by our hijackers."

"One more thing Ahmad" Howard said adamantly, "I also want you to place Spot somewhere on your person."

#

Marino was more than perturbed, he was livid. He didn't like the weasel DeWitt dictating to him how a plan was going to go. He also didn't like the fact that he believed DeWitt was playing both sides of the field—which is why he asked Allen Knox for a favor.

The fact that the sniveling little weasel gave up the information *so easily* to Knox made Marino wonder why *he* hadn't thought of putting a knife to DeWitt, instead of his bringing along Fleischman to make a deal.

He had witnesses, that's why . . . and that's the only reason.

#

Howard was quite pleased with Ahmad's invention; so was Marino. But invention aside, he was in a tight spot. If Gil Holloway *is* the leak how much information should he know about this operation? The other problem? If Gil Holloway *isn't* the leak he won't be given enough information to assist Ahmad should a tight situation occur.

I have to make a decision, he was thinking. *I could be putting their lives in jeopardy.*

#

Kilpatrick Burns, Lorna Hunter and her father and brother were sitting in Burns' apartment in Baltimore. Although summer in the city, the mood was on the chilly side in the apartment.

"Lorna, honey, me and Freddy been wondering where you been for the past couple of years? We've been look . . ."

"Why are you here Dad?" she said cutting him off.

He came to the point. "We heard you have quite a profitable business goin' here on the east coast and want to be part of it. We want to get out of the nutty stuff we been in 'cause it hasn't gotten us nowhere and thought you might want to hire family, you know, people you can trust."

She looked at him and then to her brother and then back to him. She held in her anger. "People I can trust? You think I can trust you and Freddy? In order to put money down on a Mercedes, you sold all of Mother's things before she was cold in the ground. I busted my butt every day cooking and cleaning for you two while I was trying to get through high school! I worked every angle I could to get a college scholarship because you said we didn't have any money, yet you and Freddy were walking around with diamond rings on every finger. You accelerated Mother's death and I'm never going to forgive you for that! If you and Freddy need some money Burns will see to it that you get back to wherever you came from."

She got up and went into another room.

Her father and brother got up from the couch and Burns gave each of them five hundred dollars. Her father counted his share, looked in the direction of the room she had gone into, paused for a moment, then left the apartment with Freddy not far behind. They got into their BMW and drove off. She watched from the window as the car faded away.

#

Howard was wondering where Allen Knox was when he finally received a text from him on his phone. "Cherry Hills Hotel, DuPont Circle, 217, 8p".

He hadn't seen Knox for four months since their two agencies worked together as a task force to round up a bunch of international diamond smugglers. Knox was crucial to the mission because he was a first-rate strategist, smart and always seemed keenly aware of his surroundings. Howard felt that if it hadn't been for Knox's Russian fluency and illegal arms expertise the operation might have gone bust after a few days.

They talked about life and basketball for the first 15 minutes and then the conversation went in the direction that had brought them there. The discussion centered mostly on Greg DeWitt and his knowledge of The D's operation, but it seemed no matter how long it took, both men knew they had to discuss the leak on Howard's team. They easily ruled out who it might not be, and finally the list boiled down to Gil Holloway, Richard Cruz and Michael Taylor. They decided they would devise a tactic that would force a hand.

"My perp" Knox offered, "is someone who has worked with tobacco smuggling in the past and has more than a modicum of knowledge. I'm leaning toward the boys from ATF 'cause they're some sneaky bastards."

Howard lowered his head at the statement since he felt the same way about the CIA. However for this exercise he had no choice but to trust Knox. "I don't know Knox" he said shaking his head. "Holloway and Forrestal worked, even if it was briefly, on tobacco trafficking two years ago and readily admit some knowledge of the M.O., which is why Stanton Abrams suggested their assistance on this case. I really don't want to think that it's Holloway, but you said you have an idea . . . tell me what you're thinking."

"I'm thinking that someone at ITC hates DeWitt enough that we can steer him or her to our side. Maybe this someone can be persuaded to answer some under the table questions about him. Let's see, who can it be: a jilted lover? Sexual harassment? Racism? And if this person can be trusted we would need to steer clear of DeWitt because you know of course he's playing both sides of the field?"

"That's Marino's thinking too."

Knox continued. "DeWitt is probably being paid by ITC to make sure our agencies are lured away from tobacco trafficking to concentrate on lesser crimes, like undocumented worker fallout. Nice diversion tactic. I'm anxious to find out who this new friend of ours is at ITC".

"Knox, slow your roll. First things first, like telling Marino our theory."

Once they discussed their plan with Marino calls and visits were quickly made to vendors that conducted business with ITC Tobacco. After a day of searching, nothing seemed to turn up. Then finally a bite—a disgruntled vendor who sued ITC because he believed he was repeatedly being sold shoddy tobacco for his retail shop. After complaining for a year and getting nowhere with management he decided he had no option but to sue ITC. Although it took two years of his life in court, Norbert Pike won.

Yep, that's who the agents wanted to talk to . . . and talk he did. Howard and Knox met Pike in Virginia where he told them all about the Mexicans working on the tobacco plantation that seemed to be bought lock, stock and barrel. He said their paychecks were almost totally eaten into by the company store. "They're like slaves," he said, "and I heard that if any of those Mexicans complained they were deported back to the mother ship."

"Do you know of any employees at ITC looking to get even with the company?" Knox asked casually. Pike couldn't stop smiling. "I don't believe there are ten employees in the whole damn company that are happy to be there. Sounds like Sodom and Gomorrah, doesn't it? My daughter used to work in the sales department but got fed up when they took so long to settle my case. She also worked with two *more than qualified* Hispanic women who were continually passed over as Directors. Maybe you could talk to them about ITC? I bet you they could give you a mouthful. My daughter says that one of the ladies got canned when she complained about promotion promises never materializing. Of course they said they had to let her go because of downsizing. I think she is still looking for a job. I could give you both of their names."

Norbert Pike was a godsend.

#

Alberto Marino never trusted the CIA; he had his reasons. But he was now faced with two choices: letting Knox roam freely on this maneuver, or placing him on a leash. He decided to place him on a leash . . . with Howard at the end of it. Marino was insistent with Knox that any and all information he got he had to share it with Howard. But Knox got a kick out of reminding Marino several times that *his team* sent for him, not the other way around.

Overall Marino thought Knox was a good guy. He was an excellent strategist but he could work your blind side and you'd find yourself waking up and wondering what had just happened. This was Knox's way of doing business—always working in shadows, always hiding behind closed doors, always secretive. But Knox was CIA and Marino's feelings were always going to be that this was the way they operated and that's how they worked. He had great respect for Knox's services but he could never completely trust him because he could never completely believe anything he said. What a paradox.

Knox was okay with how the FBI viewed him; it wasn't personal. They had limitations but he was willing to work around them. They were home grown and he was global. They were dangerous and he was lethal. Unfortunately they could have a family life and he could only dream about one. He liked Tim Yamamoto but he felt a special kinship with Howard Watson. Both men were fluent in Russian (Knox was also fluent in German and French), both had served in combat (years apart) and both believed they were the next Michael Jordan!

But of all the people Knox liked the most—hands down . . . Janet Forrestal.

Dilemma . . . big time.

#

Howard set up a meeting with the two disgruntled Hispanic women from ITC—Cristina Saavedra and Antonia Sanchez. The women did not want to be seen anywhere near the FBI Headquarters building so Howard and Stanley had to meet them at a convenient place for them—The Smithsonian Center for Latino Initiatives. Howard was a little impressed that these two women would drive 50 miles out of their way to be heard . . . and at the Smithsonian.

One of the women, Cristina Saavedra, was on her way to file papers with the EEOC for discrimination.

"See, I know the truth" she said. "I applied for several positions at ITC over the last five years and several times an Anglo got the job. I was always being fed a lie. Once I was told that I needed an advanced degree for a Director's position—that was crap too because the Anglo who got the job has only a bachelor's degree and I have a master's! Another thing, one of the Directors doesn't like me personally and has called me a malcontent. He even went so far as to say that I needed to "tone down (my) rhetoric about chauvinism and racism around the plant."

The other woman, Antonia Sanchez, told them that Greg DeWitt was a "butt kisser" and that she had been trying to get an appointment with him for over three months to discuss why she hadn't gotten a promotion . . . again. She then got laid off. Of course she was told "it was really due to *downsizing*".

Stanley looked over at Howard and picked up his signal. "Ms. Sanchez and Ms. Saavedra, we need your help. This is not about your employment at ITC. It is about illegal tobacco trafficking at ITC."

Sanchez looked confused. "Excuse me?" she asked. "Agent Marino said . . ."

Stanley continued. "We need your help. We need to get two of our agents into ITC in order to bust up a particular smoke ring hijacking tobacco trucks loaded with un-taxed cigarettes. Can you help us out?"

Sanchez was mute for a moment. "I have no idea what you're talking about Chief Stanley. I thought you officers were going to help us out by getting rid of Greg DeWitt or at the very least helping us . . . me get my job back. If . . ."

Howard cut her short. "Ms. Sanchez if you help us out I can pretty much guarantee you'll get your job back."

"Agent Watson, I still have no idea what you're talking about. Maybe . . ."

Cristina Saavedra broke in. "I can get your people on the assembly line. I know what you're talking about Agent Watson."

\#

Janet was feeling uneasy. She wasn't going to accept Allen Knox's invitation to dinner once he told her that only

Marino and Watson knew he was back in the States. On the other hand he did offer her an out. "If you feel like you can't go through with this, I really understand and perhaps we can get it together in a few weeks, after this case."

I should have told him no. I should have told him not-at-this-time. But I really like him. I haven't liked anyone in a long time. Allen is different enough that I don't have to be someone else with him.

They drove in separate cars and met in the parking lot of a small Italian eatery in Reston, Virginia, roughly 40 minutes from the Capitol. The restaurant was dark, but not uncomfortable. Cozy, but appropriate. She and Knox talked about everything for almost two hours . . . including her humiliation regarding her rogue FBI father.

They were just about to order dessert when Janet noticed a familiar looking woman walking into the restaurant and taking a booth in the back. Shortly thereafter a man *who was familiar to her* walked in, looked toward the back and took a seat across from the woman in the booth.

"Is something wrong Janet?" Knox asked, wiping his mouth with his napkin. "Allen" she said in an almost whisper, "don't look back but there's an ATF Agent who is working on our team making conversation with a possible suspect in our tobacco smuggling case."

Without looking Knox wanted to know if it was Agent Cruz or Taylor. Janet looked at him in amazement. "It's Agent Taylor" she said. Knox smiled and asked if he was facing her. "No" she answered. He then suggested they both leave without delay but not in a hasty manner as to cause attention. He left more than enough cash on the table and they left.

When they reached her car he told her about the leak on Howard's team. He also told her that he picked the ATF agents as the prime suspects. He didn't feel he had to mention Holloway's name. "The problem is a big one for me Janet" he said. "You see, in order for you to get a justified accommodation medal for identifying the leak you would have to tell Watson and Marino that you got the information from me because you were out with me."

#

"Howard, I know it's 11 pm" Tim said hurriedly, "but I was just thinking about the Albascanner that Ahmad invented about 12 years ago while we worked on John Mason's case. Remember it allowed us to listen to cassette tapes that we also thought were blank?"

Tim got Howard's attention; he then sat up in bed and tiredly said "yes". Next he glanced over at his wife, who gave him the look that said she was still trying to sleep. "Sorry Carol, I'll take this call in the den."

"So what are you thinking Tim?" Howard asked while closing the door to the den.

"I'm thinking since we have Knox, why don't we use him? He knows all about these types of gadgets just like Ahmad. Remember when Janet and I were imprisoned in that basement of the house with him? Do you recall that I told you he had a type of keypad in the heel of his shoe and all he had to do was press buttons to activate his coordinates? Even though we didn't get a chance to use it, Knox is one slippery, inventive dude. We need him Howard. He can probably help us with these DVD's. He can also get us someone we can trust to decode those letters. What do you say?"

"I'll send him a text in the morning and see if he can fit us into his schedule when he gets here, or whatever he calls a schedule. Maybe he'll even tell us if such an invention already exists in his world of intelligence work. Thanks for the call Tim."

Tim knew this meant goodbye. He then heard Kelly's voice.

"Tim, who are you talking to at this hour?"

"Just Howard honey; go back to sleep."

"You and Howard have something going on that Carol and I should know about?" she asked sarcastically.

"Not at this time" he answered.

#

Marino called Stanley at his office because he was curious about the conversations he and Howard had with the two women from ITC. He had to know if they were on board and if they could be trusted.

"I think so Al" Stanley was saying on the phone. "One woman just wants her job back. I don't believe she can really help us. She clearly understands the felony involved in disclosing any information about this operation. The other woman, Cristina Saavedra, is well aware of the tobacco trafficking at ITC. She has been afraid to say anything because she doesn't know how high up on the corporate ladder the operation extends. She doesn't believe anyone knows that she knows, except now for Sanchez."

"Saavedra also knows which assembly line the un-taxed cigarettes will run through but not which truck or trucks will be hijacked. She knows Greg DeWitt is behind a lot of the action. She wants him fired. She thinks maybe with him gone, her promotion might go through."

"Will she get Waverly and Holloway into ITC under the radar?"

"Yes. She is dating another employee in their HR department who is willing to help us out as long as we don't use his name. No one on the assembly line will know that Waverly and Holloway are undercover. Saavedra used to work in ITC's Maryland plant before she moved over to Virginia so the rumor mill will believe that they transferred from that division. The Warrenton plant closes daily at 4 pm so Saavedra will have both agents trained on the line this evening at 6 pm by a trustworthy supervisor. Waverly and Holloway will then be ready to go on the line tomorrow morning and be ready for Operation Canine the next day."

"Great work Stanley. Watson should be dropping by momentarily. I'd like for you to call me back then; say in 30 minutes?"

"Sure Al—no problem. I'm here all day."

"Stanley, find out about this Saavedra woman. I don't want Waverly and Holloway walking into a dead end situation."

#

When Howard arrived, Marino wanted to know whether DeWitt had given Knox any information on The D's subsequent moves.

"I talked with Knox via phone yesterday" Howard said. "He told me DeWitt spilled the beans on two upcoming jobs—one is the Warrenton Tobacco plant, and the other is the Kilgallen Tobacco plant. He also said DeWitt thinks he was recognized in the restaurant when he met up with Stanley. If that's true, whoever is the shot caller could be in the process of changing the plan. We'll see. DeWitt won't say who the rogue is. He still thinks this is leverage for him for making sure we go after the judges."

"So he's for real on this worker issue and not just using the fallout as a smokescreen?"

"Yeah Al, I do believe he is for real on this issue."

"What time will Waverly and Holloway be here?"

"I asked them to join us at 1pm. When do you want Operation Canine to proceed?"

"What do you think?"

Before Howard had a chance to answer, Marino's Executive Assistant announced that Stanley was on the line.

"Stanley, I have Watson in my office. What did you find out about the Saavedra woman?"

"Al, as far as we can tell, she is on the up and up. No priors, nor real credit issues. Two kids, divorced, master's degree in Business from U of M, College Park; drives a six year old Volvo. Ex-husband lives in Florida with new wife."

"Good work Stanley. Howard . . ."

Stanley cut him off. "Al, it's the other woman you need to know about—Sanchez."

"What about her?"

"She was arrested eleven years ago in New Mexico for trying to transport five kilos of coke out of Mexico. She was given two years prison time, five years probation because she gave up a name and the judge felt sorry for her. Get this; her ex-husband recently shared a jail cell with our Lorna Hunter's father in Arizona."

"Whoa!" was all Marino could say.

Howard broke in. "Jim this is an amazing piece of information. I'm wondering if Sanchez is part of DeWitt's effort to throw us off trafficking."

"Probably" Stanley said.

"Stanley, do you think Saavedra knows this about Ms. Sanchez?"

"Al, all we can do is ask."

#

Lorna Hunter was meeting with Burns and the rest of his crew in the Warrenton farmhouse. "Okay, listen up. As I said the ATF and FBI are on to us so we have to play it smarter. They believe we are going to hit the Warrenton plant on Friday, but the plan has changed—we're going to hit Kilgallen instead. Also, our plant said they are placing two FBI agents in the Warrenton plant as decoys. They're probably after DeWitt. Has anybody heard from him yet?"

All heads shook no.

"He'll show up" Burns said confidently. "We owe him money."

"Burns, tell me the plan."

We have two trucks to hit, both carrying 2,000 each. Darryl and Tyson will take the first truck. They'll do the bogus cop routine again. Two other boys will meet them at the junction of 42 and 128 at the abandoned old iron ore plant where some of their people will be waiting to transfer the cigarettes to our vans. Darryl will drive the truck and abandon it miles away. Tyson will pick him up."

"What about the other truck?"

"Two additional men will drive it in the opposite direction going the back way to 42 and 128. The boys will wait for them as well at the iron plant. They'll transfer the cartons same way as Darryl and Tyson. One will drive the van and abandon it miles away and the other will pick him up. Clear enough for you?"

"Pretty clear. Does everybody have cell phones?"

Everyone nodded affirmatively.

"Does everyone know how to use a cell phone?"

#

"Allen, what do you mean?"

"I mean Janet, how would you know about the leak on Watson's team? Only Watson, Yamamoto, Marino and I know about the leak. How would you explain knowing this?"

"Can't I just say I was at dinner with a friend and saw them together?"

"You could. But you would be putting yourself and your job at risk from that point on if further questioning occurs. I don't know . . . I . . . I can't let you do this."

"Allen, you're right. I can't lie. But then I really wouldn't be lying would I?"

"Who's the friend Janet? You're not from here. Who would be the friend?"

"I . . . I don't know. Maybe we should talk to Howard—he would understand; I'm sure of it."

"Janet you're not sure of it. Watson would feel he was stepping across the line. I know the feeling."

He looked straight in her eyes when he said this.

"I can't tell Watson that Agent Taylor is the leak because I don't know what Lorna Hunter looks like and Taylor could be having dinner with any woman, including his sister. You will miss your chance at an accommodation because identifying the leak is foremost on Marino's and Watson's agenda. You were perceptive enough to recall her picture and then to note why an agent might be communicating with the enemy."

"Maybe the accommodation doesn't mean as much to me as it does to you. Maybe . . ."

"Janet please. You know promotions and awards mean everything to us. It means more money, more maneuvers, more prestige; top jobs. You're going to tell me that doesn't mean anything to you? If you say no, then you are your father's daughter."

She looked at him glaringly. "That was a low blow. Goodnight Agent Knox."

He grabbed her. "Janet wait. I said that because you're *not* a liar. You have integrity, you're honest and reliable. Women in the field *and* the office look up to you. The whole reason you became an agent in the first place was because of an inner longing to be of service. Honor and awards, though, come with a price."

"Then please Allen, let me talk to Howard. We can't let Taylor win."

"Only if you promise that I will be in the room too."

Later, she found herself both actor and audience in a performance. She heard herself say yes to his invitation back to his hotel room for a drink, wondering why, but certain that it was right. He almost seemed to gulp down the scotch and when his hand touched her, it was still cold from the ice in the glass. Janet saw herself formal and disciplined in a blouse buttoned nearly to her neck. Suddenly, Knox's strong arms pulled her to him and she felt afraid, as if she were being attacked. His lips were persistent. She heard the gasp that passed her lips. As the motion grew between them, she felt the strength of him in her arms, and then more deeply within her. She closed her eyes and gave in to the rhythm, wanting nothing more than to keep the music playing.

Knox felt the tension. His body began to tighten. His mind began to focus. Somehow, this woman had gotten to him. Their small talk was almost comical as the reality of what was about to happen . . .

He wasn't sure if he moved first, or if Janet suddenly abandoned all formality. His lips pressed hard against hers. His arms encircled her. The frustratingly small buttons of her blouse finally gave way. He wasn't sure if it took forever or if it took a moment, but somewhere, between the flesh and fury, Knox knew something had changed. As he held Janet in his arms, he felt his world change. A smile crept across his face.

#

Ahmad and Holloway drove the little more than 60 minutes to the ITC plant in Warrenton. Mr. Davis, the supervisor met them at the back gate. He smiled at them and thanked them for trying "to clean up this place so the government don't shut us down. People need their jobs."

For the next two hours he trained them on all aspects of the assembly line but mostly on the area of the line that made sure all cartons had 20 packs of cigarettes in them. Ahmad could not understand how a person could do this job for eight hours a day, five to six days a week. He then thanked God for having parents who stayed on his back about getting a good education.

Holloway seemed to be getting a kick out of the machines—like a boy in a toy store. Perhaps he realized he would only be doing this job for 16 hours so it wasn't like it was going to be a backbreaking effort on his part. He couldn't believe people actually did this job for a living. He felt especially blessed that he didn't have to. He also didn't smoke so that was another feather in his cap.

Both men were surprised that they were tired when the training was over. Mr. Davis told them they had done an exceptional job. He also mentioned that they should not hold any lengthy conversations with any employees. "This is almost like high school 'round here" he said. "These folks live little lives so in here they gossip non-stop just to have something to talk about. You could listen but don't get in it. I'll make sure to check in on you routinely. See you tomorrow and good luck officers."

The agents thanked him liberally. Ahmad noticed that when he shook Mr. Davis' hands that they were heavily calloused but at the same time warm and friendly—it matched his smile.

#

The alarm on Ahmad's cell phone went off and he just knew it was wrong. *It can't be morning already?* He remembered falling into bed. He just didn't remember falling asleep.

Miles away, Holloway felt the same way. *Did someone sucker punch me in a brawl last night and I just don't remember?*

#

Howard and Stanley were sifting through donuts on Marino's desk when Tim walked in.

"Good, you're here" Marino said. "Where is Forrestal?"

Before anyone could answer Janet walked through the oak doors. A smile was on her face. Tim noticed.

"Ok, Forrestal's here, so let's get underway" Marino said. "Waverly and Holloway achieved their objective yesterday, isn't that right Howard?"

"Yes Al. As a matter of fact, they are presently slaving away at the Warrenton plant. Also, according to Gil, seems the supervisor, Mr. Davis, didn't seem to know or let on that he knew anything about our Ms. Sanchez's background, which leads me to believe that someone in a position of authority hired her."

"Okay, that's a start" Marino added. "Will Knox be in today?"

"Yes" Howard said to Marino without looking at him. "He will meet up with us today at 1pm."

"Good" Tim said smiling. "It will be good to see him again."

Janet did not say a word.

"What was Knox doing in Argentina?" Stanley asked.

"Who knows" Marino offered. "He's CIA. They only report to God."

Everyone smiled.

#

Knox met with Howard and Marino at 11am before joining the rest of the team at 1pm. He wanted to report on what he found out about DeWitt and also to connect with Jim Stanley regarding additional news on Antonia Sanchez. He told Stanley that "Sanchez not only did time in New Mexico, she was also busted seven years ago in Arizona for credit card theft."

Stanley was always amazed at the information the CIA and FBI could find that other law enforcement agencies were not privy to and this used to make him bristle . . . with jealousy. Now though, he had connections with several influential friends in both agencies so he could always get the information he needed. These friends, who included Howard, were key to his swift rise in law enforcement. His promotions, although justified, caused others to feel the way he used to feel . . . jealous.

#

Ahmad and Gil were tired after just three hours on the line. Several women in the unit gave both of them looks suggesting conversation maybe later at lunch . . . or after work? The agents tried not to be disrespectful or insensitive toward the women because they were really just trying to concentrate on getting their work done, which seemed to make the women like them even more. *Go figure.*

Mr. Davis visited them several times prior to lunch but neither agent had seen him since lunch and it was almost 4 pm. "Maybe he'll be here before we get off" Holloway said to Ahmad.

"Or maybe" Ahmad said, "he had other more pressing issues to deal with besides us."

"I don't know" Holloway said shaking his head. "He's supposed to check on us."

Thirty minutes later Ahmad and Holloway were done for the day. They decided to stop in the HR department and see if Mr. Davis was still around and had forgotten about them. When they finally found the wing of the plant that housed the HR department, the lights were out and the doors were locked; looked like everyone had gone home.

Ahmad and Gil decided they would do the same thing. Once in their vehicle they reported their day to Howard, who was quite curious about Mr. Davis' whereabouts.

"When was the last time either of you saw him?" he asked.

"He said "It's time for lunch" to me and Ahmad around noon", Holloway answered.

Ahmad added. "I thought I caught a glimpse of him going down another hall as we were heading back from lunch. He didn't acknowledge me so it might not have been him. What are you thinking Howard?" he asked.

"He might have forgotten to check on you. It happens . . . I just don't know. Did you see our Ms. Saavedra today?"

"I don't know about you Ahmad", Holloway answered, "but I didn't see her."

"I didn't see her either Gil, but remember, she said she doesn't work anywhere near this area of the facility."

"You two will have to play it cool because as I told you last night we think Sanchez is part of DeWitt's ring. Even though she is no longer at ITC we still believe the balance of her bunch still works there. I still find it very strange that you two didn't see Saavedra at lunch, or even all day", Howard said with an air of concern. "Guys, do you know what you're doing as far as placing Spot in the carton?"

"Yes, Howard" Ahmad said tiredly. "Gil and I will stop at the freezer in the lab tomorrow around 5am and pick up the twelve wafers. This way, we have a complete 72 hours of life in them."

"Good. Tim will meet you there to make sure everything goes off without a hitch. Watch your backs tomorrow. Keep Spot close. I mean it."

#

Right before their morning break, Gil heard one of the women ask another on her way to a smoke break "Cartons ready for ten?"

The other woman answered, "Yes, but the trucks won't be here until eleven."

Gil then got up from his machine and headed toward the break room. He tried listening for more talk but was drowned out by several shrill bells declaring a fire drill. He and Ahmad were surprised since Mr. Davis hadn't told them it was going to happen. As a matter of fact, Holloway had just now realized that they hadn't seen Mr. Davis this morning even though they'd been there more than two hours. The agents decided they would venture over to HR instead of going outside with the rest of the 800 employees.

As they tried to remember exactly where the HR department was located, three men stopped them in the hallway and asked them to hand over their guns. They had no guns on them but were still frisked and relieved of their wallets and cell phones.

"What's going on?" Holloway asked.

"We know you're both FBI" one of the men said. "What we don't know is how you plan on leaving?" With that both agents were told to place their hands folded on top of their heads. They were then steered to a freight elevator and taken down several levels to what looked like a large laundry area.

Once downstairs, they were shoved into an open space the size of a large bedroom. It had no windows and the only door was the one they were shoved through. It looked as if it had been someone's office at sometime in the past. It still had a desk in it and an attached bathroom. The only other things in the space were a scared Mr. Davis and a more scared Cristina Saavedra. Both were tied up and sitting in a corner with duct tape across their mouths.

"Why are they here?" Ahmad demanded. "They are just innocent bystanders. Why don't you let them go? It's really us you want."

"Oh my" one of the men said. "Innocent? C'mon you can do better than that. As soon as we find out what we're supposed to do with you two, we'll decide what to do with our other friends."

While holding a gun on Ahmad and Gil the other two men tied their hands behind their backs and duct taped their mouths.

When the men left, both agents quickly laid on the floor in fetal positions while Holloway pulled the tape off Ahmad's mouth. Ahmad then performed the same measure with Holloway, who then scooted over to Saavedra and pulled the tape off her mouth. She started crying. Ahmad pulled off Mr. Davis' tape.

The agents apologized for getting them in this predicament. "Mr. Davis, we wondered where you were yesterday when you didn't come and check on us." Holloway said.

They noticed that Mr. Davis had several bruises on his face. "I wasn't going willingly" he said as bravely as he could. Ms. Saavedra had a busted lip. "I tripped and fell when I went to the bathroom this morning" she said almost apologetically.

"How did they know that you two were our plants?"

"I guess because I told them".

The voice came from around the corner. It was Antonia Sanchez.

#

Has anyone heard from Waverly or Holloway?" Marino wanted to know.

"Not yet Al" Howard said. "Ahmad texted me about an hour ago about a fire drill at the plant and that he and Gil would go looking for Mr. Davis."

"Did they find him?" he wanted to know.

"Haven't heard yet. Janet, have you heard anything?"

"No. Gil said that after he and Ahmad talked with you last night they had a sneaking suspicion that something was up with the supervisor Davis. He said they couldn't put a finger on it."

"What about our operation? Is it still on schedule?"

Before she could answer Knox walked in. She hid her smile.

"Your people have been kidnapped" he said dryly.

"What? How do you know that Knox?" Marino asked impatiently.

"My informant at ITC told me that Waverly and Holloway were on the line before the drill but didn't return to the line after the drill. She believes . . ."

"She?" Howard asked in amazement.

"Yes, Howard, she. She's an operative working on the same assembly line as Waverly and Holloway. She just sent me a text regarding their disappearance. She believes they are somewhere in the plant. They're in serious danger. The Directive now knows they're in on their scheme. Don't know who gave their situation away."

"Do you think it was Holloway, Howard?" Marino asked.

"Al, think about it. Isn't Holloway with Ahmad?" Do you think he engineered his own kidnapping?"

Knox kept quiet. Janet kept quiet.

Agents Cruz and Taylor were announced. "Good, you're both here" Howard said. "We believe our cover has been blown at ITC?"

"How do you know that?" Cruz asked.

Janet glanced over at Taylor who caught her looking at him. The stare made him uncomfortable.

"Because Rick, they were supposed to report and they haven't."

At this moment Howard came to a strange place in his thinking. He decided that the leak was in the room. He glanced over at Knox who had the strangest look on his face.

"Cruz, you and Taylor meet Yamamoto and Knox at junction 42 and 128 in 30 minutes. Be locked and loaded. Keep your phones on vibrate and wear them on your person. We're going to get back those two agents in one piece."

"You've got it" is all Cruz said as he and Taylor headed out the door.

Howard looked over at Knox and asked "What is it you're not telling me?"

"Nothing" he said.

Janet then said, "Howard, I need to talk to you . . . privately."

"Now Janet? We have a situation here. Can it wait?

"No Howard, it can't wait."

Marino said "Knox, Yamamoto, come with me. Howard, we'll be in my office. Call us when you're ready, ok?"

Howard nodded.

#

"Antonia, what are you doing here?" Saavedra demanded.

"If you think I'm about to let you two blow a good thing for me you have me mixed up with someone else" she said.

"Ms. Sanchez, why are you doing this? Mr. Davis wanted to know. "Is it because you were let go?"

"Please. I was not let go. I just moved on to a more profitable side of the business. I'm just taking care of business."

Moments later the gang members returned and placed the tape back on the four hostages' mouths. They were all escorted through the basement of the plant to a garage area. An Escalade drove up and the four people were shoved into the waiting vehicle. The woman in the front passenger seat was talking to someone on the phone.

"Yeah, it's me. What do I do with them? What? Ok."

When she stopped talking she said to the driver "Silver Spring."

#

Janet was about to do something even she couldn't believe she could do—lie to her boss.

Howard was surprised when she said that she really needed to talk with him. He had no idea what was coming up next.

"Howard, I can't explain why I feel this way, but I think we have a mole among us."

He looked at her and really couldn't believe she was saying this. He almost couldn't get the words out of his mouth. "What makes you think that Janet?"

"Because I was out with two sorority sisters in Reston and I saw Agent Taylor with Lorna Hunter at a restaurant. I recognized Hunter from the picture we were shown and I don't believe they were talking sports. Because our operation was exposed last week and we can't seem to explain why I believe Agent Taylor might have tipped off someone. Also, he was supposedly at the dentist the day of our combined meeting but I saw him the next morning at the motel diner and his jaw wasn't swollen. I thought it odd that it was suddenly swollen when he met with us just hours later. One more thing Howard, when Gil and I worked on tobacco trafficking two years ago, Agent Taylor was the supervisor in charge of that investigation."

Knox didn't know how or what Janet told Howard but when she emerged from his office she had a slight smile on her face.

Howard hurried into Marino's office. "Thanks to Agent Forrestal, I do believe we have found our leak".

#

PART THREE

Janet was determined to find Ahmad and Gil.

She had to because she felt it was only fair. They rescued her, Knox and Tim on their last case together and it was only fitting that they should have a woman that is, Janet, rescue them now.

She somehow knew that when she woke up from this dream Ahmad and Gil would be at their regular meeting, half listening to her, as usual.

Her dream descended into a nightmare when she found out the agents were now being held hostage somewhere. Although the agents had accomplished their goal on the assembly line by placing the microchips in the cigarette cartons, the FBI task force was only able to trace eleven of the twelve cartons to two panel trucks along route 42 and 128. They arrested the four men trying to run from the vehicles. For some strange reason they couldn't find the twelfth carton.

Howard and Tim were extremely pleased that Spot worked just like Ahmad imagined it would. But where is Ahmad? Where is Gil?

Howard and Marino wanted to arrest Taylor right after they kicked the living shit out of him. Knox explained to them *no can do* because now that they know the leak was Taylor they didn't have to bargain with DeWitt any longer. Now they could just arrest him . . . unless he *wanted* to tell them where the agents were being held.

"Let's say we know where they are" Marino reasoned. "We mention this in our task force meeting with Cruz and Taylor present. If you guys can hold in your anger and put on your acting robes I believe we can give Taylor his own rope. Also, Knox, I want you to haul in DeWitt. Bring Yamamoto up to speed and take him with you."

"Sure thing" he said as he headed out the door.

"Forrestal" Marino added, "You and Howard stay. Once the other agents had departed, Marino looked exhausted. "I've got a feeling that our hostages are on their way to the Silver Spring abandoned warehouse that Waverly and Holloway found. Taylor wasn't around when our guys returned from Silver Spring, remember? So he doesn't know that we know that place exists."

Janet had a plan.

"Chief, if we pick up Taylor I can get to Lorna Hunter. I could try to get her to hire me. Being a Black woman might be in my favor . . . she might trust me. It would be no problem in finding out all the info I would need on her. I . . ."

"No", Marino said emphatically. We already have two agents in deep trouble. I haven't even told Fleischman yet. He'll say no too."

"Why?" Janet asked. "Please don't say it's because I'm a woman."

Howard jumped into the fray. "Al, it's gotta be Janet. It makes sense. Now that we know Cruz isn't the leak, he can back her up. Besides, Cruz said one of his informants infiltrated The Links gang. Maybe he can lead the way for Janet. Al, we don't have that much time to waste. Ahmad and Gil are on somebody else's hourglass."

"I . . . I don't know Howard. You and I know John; he's from the old school. I'm sorry Janet but I have to broach this subject not only with him but with Stanton. Give me a day, ok?"

What am I supposed to say "no?"

#

Lorna Hunter was somewhat guarded with Kim Miller until she saw her math skills.

"Why in the hell are you in this business?" she asked her.

"Because a B&E got me in trouble about three years ago and I had to move from California 'cause I couldn't find a job with a felony on my resume."

"What were you breaking and entering?"

"Too much to mention besides, is this a test?" Miller asked. "Can we move on? You want me to work for you or not?" She started walking away.

103

"Hey, I need to know the people around me."

"Well, I don't know about you either."

"I thought you said you knew my brother?" she snapped back.

"I said I dated him once in high school. Know him? Please. I hope you don't mind my being blunt but your brother and your father have reputations as big mouths. I heard that you were doin' a boomin business so here I am. I can't go back to The Links 'cause they were all taken into custody by the Feds. I luckily got out three weeks before the surprise round up. I left them because they kept cutting my action."

Lorna had done her homework by having the new hire checked out. For some strange reason she couldn't find Taylor, so she used her other informant who had also belonged to The Links gang. He said he thought he recalled her. "Black chick, red hair? She was the numbers girl if I remember" he said. That was good enough for Hunter.

The so-called informant was actually an undercover ATF agent who had infiltrated The Links tobacco ring and assisted in the surprise arrest by the Feds. He supplied all the info on Kim Miller—Janet's new alias.

#

Rick Cruz felt personally to blame when told about Michael Taylor's defection to the dark side. Although he told his superiors that he would not let Taylor know he was aware of his desertion of duty, he would also not take part in his arrest. Cruz also went on to say that he would make every effort to ensure Agent Forrestal's back was thoroughly protected.

#

Howard and Marino met up with Stanley in his office in Maryland. "What we can't do is go to pieces just because we haven't heard from Waverly and Holloway in 18 hours. Ahmad will certainly think of something."

"I wish I were as confident as you are Jim" Howard said soberly. "And now we have Janet out there by herself."

"Well she's not by herself Howard. Rick Cruz is around."

"True Jim, I just meant that . . .

He was interrupted by a phone call for Stanley.

"Just a second, he's right here." Stanley then gave the phone to Marino. "Al, it's for you; Yamamoto."

"Yeah Tim. What?"

He looked at Howard. "DeWitt was found bound and gagged in his motel room. They got there just in time because the fool is still alive."

Marino, Howard and Stanley waited for Tim and Knox to arrive at Stanley's office. While they waited Stanley was able to get the complete details of the attempted murder.

"Tape was on his mouth and nostrils. The rope found around his arms and legs indicated a struggle. Somebody wanted him dead. Who knew he was there?"

"I thought only me and Knox". Marino said. "Obviously I was wrong."

#

The white panel truck pulled up in front of an abandoned warehouse. The two drivers pulled the four people out of the back. They were bound and gagged. Ahmad looked around and realized he and Holloway had been there before. He couldn't imagine where they could possibly hide them since there were no doors and no separate rooms.

The four hostages were ushered inside the warehouse. Suddenly one of the henchmen pushed a bale of hay aside and a trap door in the floor appeared. The man opened the trap door and went down the stairs first, followed by the four hostages and then the last man holding a gun on them.

The room was huge. Cigarette cartons lined every wall. Ahmad guessed there must have been over 25,000 cartons of cigarettes in the room. He now knew that after seeing all of this, whoever was in charge wasn't going to let any of them live.

"Now what are we possibly going to do with all of you?" said a voice familiar to Ahmad and Gil. They were shocked to learn that the voice belonged to ATF Agent Michael Taylor. It then became clear to both Ahmad and Gil that Taylor had betrayed them all along.

#

Spot sent a text to the microchip recorder listing coordinates. "How is this possible Tim?" Howard asked. "We retrieved all of the cartons."

"It's Janet, Howard. She's giving us her coordinates."

"Forrestal is on a mission by herself?" Knox asked.

"Yes Knox" Marino answered. "Forrestal is out there. It was her call, and strangely enough Fleischman, as well as Stanton Abrams gave her the go-ahead."

"Is she strapped?" He wanted to know.

Howard's antenna went up. "She has a weapon fastened to her ankle. She's wearing jeans that fit inside her boots. Also, one of Ahmad's lab assistants made her a chip and it's inside the heel of her boot . . . which is how we were able to pick up her coordinates. Another thing, she's not alone because the only way she got approval was because Rick Cruz said he would watch her."

Knox's mind went into overdrive. He was careful not to show it on his face.

Howard then realized Knox had a thing for Forrestal. "Ain't that a bitch", he said to himself. He wanted to smile but suddenly realized the mission could be compromised if Knox decided to take it upon himself to go rescue Forrestal. "This is how CIA worked", he was thinking. "Always assuming they don't need any help". He had to talk with him.

Before he got the chance Marino beat him to the punch.

"Knox" Marino said looking at a map, "pull up these coordinates and tell us what we're looking at."

Knox figured out the coordinates within minutes. "Four miles west of Warrenton, Virginia, off Lee Highway 234, about 40 miles south of Reston. When we pull up this

Google map it shows only a farmhouse. That's probably it. What do you want to do?"

Ten minutes later Spot sent another text. Knox again looked up the coordinates and said "Different coordinates. Now it's saying her position is 15 miles north of Silver Spring, Maryland, which is about 50 miles north of Warrenton. She can't possibly be in both places within 10 minutes. No way."

Howard's mind was racing. "Knox pull up the Google map again, see what it points to."

"It's pointing to a warehouse Howard. Is this the same one Holloway and Waverly said they visited?"

"Yes, I do believe that is the home of Zephyr, Inc."

"But didn't Holloway say that it was virtually empty, the doors didn't close and the roof had holes in it? Where could they possibly be holding them?"

"Howard" Tim asked, "what if Ahmad is wearing a chip too? Didn't you tell him to also place a chip on his person?"

"Wow, Tim, that's brilliant. I forgot about that. Maybe that's why we couldn't find the twelfth carton because Ahmad has the chip on him."

"The question as I see it" Tim asked, "is what took so long for Ahmad's chip to emerge?"

"The question as I see it" Knox added, "is which chip is Janet's and which chip is Ahmad's?"

#

Ahmad was hoping Howard or Tim looked at the Spot recorder before he and the others were shepherded underground. If they did, they would know their exact location. He was pretty happy with himself for placing the last chip inside his boxer shorts. He almost forgot but at the last minute remembered that Howard had requested it. Later when the men made him and Gil strip down to their underwear they didn't find anything.

He wondered where Davis and Saavedra were. He was really praying that nothing happened to either of them, since it was his and Gil's fault that they got caught up in this situation. Although he didn't have a cell phone or watch on him he knew their time was running out, especially with Spot. He figured they had about 40 hours left if they were to be found alive.

Holloway felt just as terrible about how the deal went down. The terrified look on the faces of Mr. Davis and Ms. Saavedra had said it all. He was hoping that Marino or Watson got Ahmad's chip information. He hadn't realized that Ahmad followed up on Howard's request to place a chip on his person. He knew The Directive wasn't going to free any of them without some major guarantees. *They'll probably let the civilians go but not me or Ahmad, without one of us, or both of us, getting killed.*

\#

One of Ahmad's lab assistants called Tim to tell him that they could finally view the DVD's.

"Wow" Tim said. "That's good news. He looked over at Knox giving him the thumbs up because his CIA operative came through with a machine already in place to read so-called blank tapes.

Howard, Tim, Knox, Stanley and Fleischman all met in Marino's conference room. The video looked as if it was being recorded without anyone's knowledge, except, of course, for the person recording the conversation.

Ronny Stacktrain was seated at a table in a room with Greg DeWitt and Superior Court Judges Robert Keppler and Paul Creighton. Also seated were top Maryland attorneys Willard Stockton and Daniel McCormick.

> **Stacktrain**: Judge Keppler, you can't possibly believe that reporters won't find out about this?

> **Robert Keppler**: Major Stacktrain, we're here because these people who came to you with their lies about the ITC organization should be deported. All they want to do is start trouble. We're not here to quibble about rights for these people, they aren't even Americans, yet they want to cause trouble here in America.

> **Stacktrain**: What does that mean? That all you white folks who came across the

water in the beginning of the 20th century suddenly want to close the door on everyone else? No one else is allowed into America?

Paul Creighton: No, Major, that's not what Bob means.

Stacktrain: Your Honor, please enlighten me. What exactly does Judge Keppler mean?

Keppler: I mean these people, these Mexicans, are not Americans. They don't belong here and yet they come to our country to work, have American babies so they can stay and then don't pay taxes or social security. When they abuse the privilege of working in our country we must usher them out. We must.

Creighton: Ron, may I call you Ron?

Stacktrain: No you may not Judge Creighton.

Creighton: Okay then, Major. These people . . . work in our fields, get fed, have a roof over their heads, and are able to send their children to American schools while they work. Then they turn their backs on the very people who allowed them into the country in the first place and stab them in the back.

Stacktrain: You mean because the people that let them into the country couldn't care less if they dropped dead in the fields after working 12-15 hours a day, or require medicine if stung by a bee and happened to be allergic to bee stings, or even, heaven forbid, just need a 15 minute water break every now and then from the penetrating sting of the sun? You mean these people?

Daniel McCormick: Major, yes *these* people. It's hard to believe you're this naïve. All we want from you is your word that the complaints brought to you will be disposed of permanently. You of course will be paid handsomely. I'm slightly curious though as to why these people brought their complaints to a Major General in the Marines in the first place.

Greg DeWitt: They didn't. They brought the complaints to his wife who teaches some of their kids.

Stacktrain glared at DeWitt.

Stacktrain: It doesn't matter *how* I found out, it still doesn't excuse the abuses toward these workers. If you're gonna treat them like shit, why hire them? You just don't stop do you? Take a look around this room gentlemen. Do you remember when we used to be called Polack, Jew, Wop, Mick, Chinaman or Nigger? No, I guess you don't remember that. This is how we used to be treated and now you want to make new slaves and call them Mexicans? You guys make me sick. Don't bother to see me out, I know my way.

When Stacktrain left the room, the conversation continued.

Keppler: Make sure no one is listening.

DeWitt got up and came back several moments later. "No one is here but us."

Keppler: What are we going to do with Stacktrain?

Creighton: How about giving this job to Taylor? He's ATF; he knows how to take care of messes like these.

Willard Stockton: Look, I don't want any part of this. I agreed to have a conversation with Stacktrain only because I'm a Board member of ITC, but nothing else. He is an upstanding gentleman and we'll just have to find another way to deal with our workers' complaints. I'm leaving.

McCormick: Sit down Willard. We're all Board members. Nobody's going to harm the Major . . . unless he doesn't back off saying he's going to the media. We just want him to dispose of those letters and not report this to the press.

Stockton: What if he says no?

McCormick: Taylor will deal with it.

The men got up from the table and left the room. Someone turned off the light in the room but the tape kept going. For the next 12 minutes the tape was recording and then someone turned it off. This someone had mailed it and another tape to a post office box in Silver Spring, Maryland.

The room took on an eerie quietness as the agents digested what they'd heard. The ringing of Marino's wall phone brought them all out of an unbearable state of disgust.

"What's on the other tape?" Howard wanted to know.

"I'm almost afraid to watch" Tim said but he still turned on the tape. Meaningless marks and words played across the screen for five minutes.

"Howard" Knox whispered loudly, "You know of course this is code, right?"

"Knox" Marino said just as loudly, "Get your decoder here pronto!"

#

Janet had no idea where she was but she believed she was at the Warrenton farmhouse. All she was hired to do was count cartons of cigarettes with the men. She was comforted by the fact that Cruz was not far away and perhaps Howard and Marino picked up her coordinates. She and a couple of men were on their way to take inventory of a shipment she was almost sure was delivered by the drivers from the ITC hijacking. When they got to the van, it was empty. One of the men immediately called someone on his cell phone. "Sir" he said, the truck is empty. "Yes sir, I'm sure it's our truck."

The voice at the other end said to look around and check to see if anyone is in the vicinity or if anyone is taking pictures!

The man looked around and told the voice on the phone, "No, I don't see nobody, just trees."

When they returned to the farmhouse Janet thought she was going to lose her lunch. Standing near the entrance of the farmhouse was Kilpatrick Burns, whom she and Holloway arrested several years ago in Philadelphia. *Oh my God, what if he remembers me?*

He was talking to two of the men when she walked by. "Excuse me miss, I don't believe we've met? He then lifted her hand and kissed it. He was about to say something else when Lorna Hunter called him. "Burns, I need to talk to you!" He looked at Janet and said "later".

"Who's the new chick?" he asked Hunter once inside the farmhouse.

"Kim Miller; she's our new numbers person; came to us through our guy from The Links. Listen up. What happened to the ITC inventory?"

"What do you mean what happened to it? Didn't Darryl and Tyson pick it up?"

"When they got to the truck it was empty."

"What did Taylor say?"

"I haven't been able to talk to him. Have you seen or heard from him?"

"Not since he picked up those two FBI agents that he's holding in the old iron ore plant. What do you suppose he's going to do with them?"

"I don't know but I hope it doesn't involve death. I don't need that kind of rap."

"For some strange reason she looks familiar" Burns said. "Don't know why."

"As many women as you've had in your life I would consider it a miracle if you could recall just one woman's name."

He was quiet for a moment.

"That's what I thought" she said in an almost disgusted tone.

All he could say was "whatever."

#

Knox's operative met him, Howard and Tim in Marino's office within two hours. Trent looked as if he was only 17 but Knox assured them he'd been a decoder for at least 10 years. He studied the letters and concluded that they were code. "It's pretty elementary" he said, "like a game".

"What do you mean a game Trent?" Howard asked.

"Because it has limited number of marks and signs to make it easy to decipher for an amateur. It's too easy not to solve in say, 2-3 minutes with a code sheet. The only problem is how the person set up the alphabet. Have you gone through the letters to see if there is a code sheet?"

The agents looked through all the correspondence that was in the file. Then it hit Knox. "We also have this same type of coding on a videotape. Can you look at it and tell us if the tape is the decoder?" Trent said "I'll try".

After viewing the tape, he concluded that it was probably the decoder.

"The series of numbers correspond to letters in the alphabet and marks and signs. Both are jumbled around to make solving difficult, but not impossible. The marks and signs are easily found on a computer keyboard, in this case though, an advanced keyboard was used in order to make more marks and signs. Why? It keeps the game from getting boring and it keeps the game going."

"So let's take a stab at the first letter".

5 4 15 14; 15 4 9; 26 12 24 14 20;—iron ore plant
42, 128;—?
20 4 24 26; 18 15 15 4;—trap door

Howard, Marino and Tim had no idea what this meant. Knox decided he would try it. "What does the 42, 128 mean since the alphabet only goes up to 26?"

Trent didn't take long with an answer. "Because this is pretty uncomplicated it could mean street numbers, route numbers, highway numbers . . ."

Howard cut him off. "Knox, look this up on Google maps. Is there an iron ore plant at routes 42&128?"

Knox quickly checked the coordinates. "No Howard, only the warehouse outside Silver Spring."

"Why don't you Google it and see what the warehouse or land used to be?" Trent asked. Howard felt he was worth whatever they weren't paying him.

"It was an iron ore plant that stored ammunition underground during the Civil War. So the warehouse must have a trap door." Knox deduced.

"And since it is underground" Tim added quickly, "This must be where Ahmad and Gil are being held. It now makes sense why we are not able to get Ahmad's coordinates."

Marino could be silent no longer. "Where the hell did Stacktrain learn how to do this?" he asked.

"If he has kids" Trent said unemotionally, "it's probably from a game, like "Detective Relentless".

Howard almost fainted. "My kids have that game! As a matter of fact, Ronny's daughters play this game with my sons all the time."

"Well obviously Major Stacktrain played this game with his daughters as well. Do you want me to decode the rest of the letters?" Trent asked.

Marino said "Most definitely."

#

Holloway was assessing his and Ahmad's whereabouts. He realized that they were being held in some type of old plant. What type, he couldn't tell. He could smell what he believed to be iron but wasn't quite sure. He was wondering if he tried to use his heel phone underground would the signal go through. He would try, but first he had to go to the bathroom.

He was lead to a primitive looking room with a stall and a toilet. The rope was removed from his wrists because *no one* wanted to hold him while he pee'd. He stepped into the stall and dialed Howard's number. It would not transmit.

"Hurry up in there!" the gang member yelled. Holloway then did his business, flushed the toilet with his foot and the rope was placed on his wrists again. He re-joined Ahmad and gave him the look that said "no go". They had to think of something else.

#

It only took Trent an hour to decode all of the letters. The agents thanked him profusely. Marino promised that the FBI would take care of him financially. Trent was most happy as he was really doing the favor for Allen Knox, his hero.

The decoded letters were put in sequential order by Trent:

> Major General Stacktrain had returned home from a two-week reconnaissance mission when he was approached by several of his wife's students' parents. They were all Mexicans who worked on the ITC plantation and were being mistreated. They complained to the union leader who contacted several persons of authority in law enforcement. They noticed that many of them who complained were soon arrested and deported, including their children. The union leader was then granted an audience with the State Rep who did absolutely nothing. Finally, they got in touch with Major General Stacktrain of the United States Marines. They thought surely he could do something.
>
> Stacktrain called Greg DeWitt, a senior level executive in HR for ITC. He made it

clear to DeWitt that he would be contacting the press and the ATF about the human abuses at ITC if DeWitt did not sit down with him. DeWitt agreed to the meeting; however he wanted Stacktrain to meet with some of the Board of ITC first. Stacktrain agreed. The meeting did not go well at all. DeWitt suggested one more meeting but it would have to be somewhere outside ITC and Quantico. Stacktrain suggested the Capital Hill Westin. DeWitt had had a change of heart. Something inside him shifted. He would now agree to speak to a reporter that Stacktrain felt they could trust with the story. When DeWitt got to the hotel, Stacktrain was already dead. ATF Taylor and an accomplice were let into the hotel room by Stacktrain who was told that DeWitt had invited them. But DeWitt had not.

This was all written in code, but by whom?

#

Janet tried her best to stay away from Kilpatrick Burns all day. It was now turning dusk and it had been a long day. She had counted and invoiced more than 10,000 cartons of cigarettes and she was dog tired. She was heading back to her truck when Burns approached her.

"Why do I feel as if I know you?" he asked.

"I don't know. Ever been in California?" she answered with confidence.

"No, I haven't" he answered.

"Okay, well that's where I'm from."

"It'll come to me" he said as he walked off.

Janet needed a drink. She was getting in her truck when Burns slithered up to her and said "You're a cop. And not just a cop, you're FBI. I remember now, Philadelphia. He pulled out his gun and then tried pulling her out of the truck by her hair. "Get out of the truck" he demanded.

Janet was getting out of the truck when she . . . slammed the door into him knocking his gun out of his hand. She kicked him in his groin, picked up his gun, reached in the back of her truck, got the duct tape and placed it over his mouth while dragging him into the woods. When he started to recover she hit him over the head with a brick. He was completely knocked out.

She got rope from her vehicle. She tied him up. She then backed her truck into the woods and with all her strength she dragged his sorry ass into the back of her truck. Her cell phone fell out of her jacket pocket and fell to the ground hitting a rock. It broke into pieces. She picked up the various parts, hopped in the truck and drove away. It was getting dark so she had to rely on the GPS in the truck.

She was hoping someone, anyone, had picked up her coordinates. She now felt she had seen enough of The D's operation that she could rest assured that Lorna Hunter and

Kilpatrick Burns will go to jail for a lengthy time. *But where is Ahmad? Where is Gil? I've got to find them. They must be at Silver Spring.* She headed in that direction with Burns in the back.

If he comes to, I'll hit him again.

#

It was almost 9 pm and Tim had dozed off on Howard's couch in his office. Spot woke him up. "The coordinates have changed" he said almost excitedly. "Knox, tell me what we're looking at."

Knox was reading in a chair. He instantly looked up the coordinates. "Whoever it is and I'm betting it's Janet, the vehicle is heading toward Silver Spring."

"Why doesn't she use her phone?" Howard asked while yawning.

"Probably no cell service" Knox reasoned.

"Wrong Knox," Howard responded. "That cell phone works everywhere, even underwater. It is its own satellite. Something must have happened to it."

"How did she get away?" Tim asked.

"It doesn't matter Tim, let's get going and meet her at Silver Spring."

#

As Janet's truck was going around a bend another truck pulled across the road blocking her path. In addition to her own gun she had Burns' gun sitting on the seat.

It was Rick Cruz.

"Remind me never to make you mad" he said. "You want me to haul Burns' ass in and come up with various charges until we can really keep him glued to a cell?"

"Rick that would be terrific. Here's the gun he pulled on me. I'm headed to Silver Spring because I now know that's where Gil and Ahmad are being held. I just hope it's not too late."

Cruz pulled Burns out of the truck. He was groggy but was able to walk to Cruz's car where he was handcuffed to a backseat door. "What happened to your phone, Janet?"

"I dropped it back at Warrenton when I was haulin' Burns into the truck. I have GPS. I can make it. Also, I still have a chip in my boot so the guys know where I'm heading."

"Alright, take care, I mean it. I'm going to call Watson and let him know your ETA. Good job."

"Bye Rick."

#

She drove as fast as she could without becoming reckless. When she got within a mile of the Silver Spring warehouse she put the truck in neutral and coasted. She parked the truck off the road. She walked uneasily through the woods. She quickly ran back to her truck to retrieve her binoculars and her softball bat. She got within 50 yards of the plant when she noticed Lorna Hunter talking to a man. She tried focusing in on what they were saying. Although she could read lips, neither of them was facing her. She heard a crunch behind her. Two men were coming her way. She ducked behind a large tree. They moved past her. She watched as they retrieved two people, a man and a woman from the warehouse. *Where did they come from? The warehouse has no doors or anything inside?* The man lit a cigarette. Lorna Hunter walked the woman into the woods. Minutes later both of them walked out. *She must've had to go to the bathroom.* The men walked both of them back into the warehouse.

I've got to see where they go!

Janet made her move around the trees being careful not to step on any broken branches or dried leaves. She saw one of the men move a bale of hay and lean down and pull up an opening of some sort on the floor! *That's where they've got them!*

#

"Where is her location now Knox?" Tim asked.

"Looks like the coordinates stop at the warehouse in Silver Spring."

Fifteen minutes later they got within 200 feet of the warehouse so Tim put the van in neutral and let it coast as far as it could go. It was then that they saw Janet's truck. The agents pushed their vehicle off the road and parked it behind the largest tree they could find. They were all locked and loaded. They navigated slowly through the trees, stopping only if they heard something. Twice it was a deer. Just then three men came out of the warehouse and started smoking.

Janet seized this opportunity to duck behind the farm equipment, lumber and other junk in the yard. She then moved smoothly into the warehouse and to the opening on the floor hoping that all the men had come out. She was in luck. They had.

At the bottom of the stairs she saw Mr. Davis and Ms. Saavedra. She put her finger to her lips to make them understand silence. She journeyed more into the massive room and then she saw them . . . Ahmad and Gil. They were alive! She ran over to them quickly and helped remove the cords around their wrists and the tape from their mouths. She observed that Ahmad's lip was swollen, he had a black eye and his arm appeared to be broken. Gil had a black eye as well. His ankle was fractured. Mr. Davis helped Gil up the stairs and she helped Ahmad. Ms. Saavedra was not far behind.

Ahmad had a plan.

As Howard and the other agents were about to ambush the three men who were smoking, a truck pulled up with three other men in tow. The shift was about to change. The odds were now steeper than before. Perhaps they should wait until the shift changed.

Suddenly they heard a woman scream. All six of the gang members fled into the warehouse and down the stairs. Janet ran to the men's truck and drove it over the opening in the floor. The men couldn't get out.

After watching this scene play out Howard radioed for assistance and gave his coordinates, and then he and Knox ran to Janet, Ahmad and Gil. Howard noticed the agents had been badly beaten. He held in his anger. *The bastards really had their way with them.*

The four people were now safe. Tim ran and got the van. He put Mr. Davis and Ms. Saavedra in it.

Two Sherriff's police cars and a State Police car arrived shortly on the scene.

Howard had a conversation with the cops. He then took Janet's bat from her and told one of the cops to move the truck. Janet yelled "No Howard! Don't do it. You'll be just like them!"

Knox was on Howard's side but pulled the bat from Howard's grip.

It took more than a minute for Howard to regain his composure. Tim had to help him walk off his anger. When they returned a few minutes later Howard looked at Janet. "You've done a great job again!"

"It was Ahmad's plan" she said sheepishly. "Last night he said he watched those men change shift but they left the keys in the truck because those getting off for the night used the same truck. In the morning another crew took the same truck. So they always left the keys in the ignition. We banked on that."

"Janet" Knox said trying not to smile too much, "You are a credit to the department . . . in many ways." She smiled deeply. She so much wanted him to take her in his arms. She knew *that* wasn't gonna happen!

Howard took the Bluetooth from his ear. "DeWitt died".

#

EPILOGUE

**Mr. Davis and Ms. Saavedra were
shaken but not stirred.**

They managed to limp to the waiting van that whisked
them from the Silver Spring warehouse. While Howard and
the rest of the crew made sure all the gang members were
loaded in police vehicles, Tim drove Davis and Saavedra to
a hospital in Silver Spring. The only thing the two wanted
to know was if their jobs were still waiting for them? Tim
chuckled and assured them that" not only are your jobs still
intact but the President of the Board of Directors and the
CEO of ITC are planning a heroes' welcome for both of you.
And yes, Ms. Saavedra, you got the promotion."

#

Fleischman, as usual, did not read his report and wanted
to hear what happened to the men in the room. Marino
grabbed a cup of coffee and repeated the story for the second
time:

"Judges Paul Creighton and Robert Keppler and attorneys Willard Stockton and Daniel McCormick were all arrested on accessory to murder charges (DeWitt and Stacktrain), kidnapping, theft with attempt to deliver an illegal product (un-taxed cigarettes) and a host of other crimes the D.A. was digging up. They were stripped of their positions and all four law licenses were revoked. They cannot post bail. Presently they are each looking at life in prison." Marino then chuckled. "No doubt all four will appeal their sentences."

Fleischman looked pleased. He looked very pleased.

"What about the haul?"

"ATF and DEA said that over 50,000 cartons of un-taxed cigarettes were found in both warehouses. This is worth over $15million street value that will never see the light of day—one of the largest hauls of tobacco smuggling to date!"

Fleischman's smile kept getting bigger.

"What about Hunter and her gang?" he asked.

"Lorna Hunter was arrested, pled guilty to kidnapping charges, conspiracy to commit cargo theft, conspiracy to transport stolen property in interstate commerce, and delivery of an illegal product. She then gave up names of her accomplices—including Michael Taylor who she said unintentionally killed Stacktrain but intentionally murdered DeWitt. She's looking at 15 years in prison. We can now say she is her father's child."

#

Michael Taylor was arrested along with Lorna Hunter at her apartment in Reston, Virginia. Cruz's men took both into custody. Cruz found very little to smile about as he watched from a distance both Taylor and Hunter being led down the stairs of her apartment building into the waiting ATF issued squad cars.

Antonia Sanchez was also arrested as she and several of her ITC bunch tried to flee in a car headed toward the West Virginia mountain range.

#

"Howard?" Tim asked. "Who do you think sent the tapes to the post office? And who turned off the videotape?"

"Stanley said before DeWitt died he told him *he* was the person who turned off the tape. He then sent the tapes and complaint letters to Stacktrain's post office box for safekeeping. Before the meeting with Stacktrain at the Westin he was supposed to bring those complaint letters to the meeting with the reporter from the *Post* but he couldn't readily find his key to the box which made him late to the meeting. When he got to the hotel he saw Agent Watson banging on Stacktrain's door and then he realized Michael Taylor had gotten there before him and Watson. DeWitt said all Stacktrain was trying to do was help people fight what looked like to them a losing battle. He was an upright guy with integrity. DeWitt said he asked Stacktrain why was he helping these people and Stacktrain told him "the first law is that you never leave a man on the battlefield."

#

The teams were gathered in John Fleischman's conference room. He looked at Marino then over at Janet. "Agent Forrestal, I want to recommend you, with Agents Marino, Abrams and Watson's endorsement, for the FBI Medal for Meritorious Achievement. Your decisive, exemplary act in the discovery of a rogue agent, and your subsequent quick thinking in the field, resulted in the protection and saving of not only our two agents' lives, but just as importantly, our two civilians' lives. Stanton Abrams will present you with your award at next month's academy graduation. We want to thank you for a job well done."

The applause was long and loud. Fleischman, Marino and Abrams shook her hand vigorously. Howard and Tim grabbed her and hugged her. Rick Cruz still managed to smile even with the disappointing news regarding his former partner. Marino hated very personal moments like this. They made him feel awkward. He hated feeling awkward.

Ahmad, his arm in a cast and Holloway, whose ankle was heavily bandaged, were incredibly proud of her. Janet looked over at Allen Knox and smiled the smile she hoped would reel him in.

Knox was in.

END